VALENTINE DREAMS

Dear Jill,

I'm so bummed. Valentine's Day is coming up and I have no valentine! You're so lucky to have Ryan. Even my mom has a valentine (if you can count Roger as a valentine—personally, I'm not so sure).

Well, at least I have the Nationals! I'm going to concentrate on skating my best. I'd love to come home with a medal—yeah, right! Wish me luck!

Love,
Tori

Super Edition #1

RINKSIDE
ROMANCE

Melissa Lowell

Created by Parachute Press

A SKYLARK BOOK
NEW YORK · TORONTO · LONDON · SYDNEY · AUCKLAND

With special thanks to Darlene Parent, director of Sky Rink Skating School, New York City.

RL 5.2, 009–012

RINKSIDE ROMANCE
A Skylark Book / February 1996

Skylark Books is a registered trademark of Bantam Books, a division of Bantam Doubleday Dell Publishing Group, Inc. Registered in U.S. Patent and Trademark Office and elsewhere.

Silver Blades™ is a trademark of Parachute Press, Inc.

Series design: Barbara Berger

ISBN 0-553-48369-2

Published simultaneously in the United States and Canada

PRINTED IN THE UNITED STATES OF AMERICA

OPM   0 9 8 7 6 5 4 3 2 1

Super Edition #1

Dear Jill,

I'm so bummed. Valentine's Day is coming up and I have no valentine! You're so lucky to have Ryan. Even my mom has a valentine (if you can count Roger as a valentine—personally, I'm not so sure).

Well, at least I have the Nationals! I'm going to concentrate on skating my best. I'd love to come home with a medal—yeah, right! Wish me luck!

Love,
Tori

Images flickered across the screen that hung from the ceiling of the plane. But Tori Carsen was much too excited to concentrate on the movie. She tore off her headphones and stared out the window. Clouds rushed by below the plane. She could hardly believe she was on her way to San Jose, California, to the U.S. National Figure-Skating Championships! Was it really happening?

How many times had she dreamed about this? Studying other skaters on TV, Tori had imagined how it would feel to be out there herself with millions of people watching. For years she had talked about it, prepared for it, and skated hard. And now it was actually happening.

"In an amazing upset in the Junior events, Tori Carsen from Seneca Hills, Pennsylvania, takes home the gold!" Tori imagined herself on the winner's podium. A medal was placed around her neck. Television cameras and newspaper reporters swarmed over her.

She had replayed this scene hundreds of times in her mind, starting when she was a seven-year-old beginning skater. Since she was eight years old, Tori had been a member of Silver Blades. It was one of the top skating clubs in the country. She and the other twenty-five members of the club practiced skating twice a day, every day but Sunday. Tori was glad to start early practice at five-thirty each morning and return to the ice after school for an afternoon session. All that practice brought her closer to her goal—more than anything, she wanted to be a champion.

Tori had been skating competitively for five years. This was the first time she had qualified for the Nationals, skating in the Junior division. Oh, she knew she didn't have much chance of winning a medal. Not this time, anyway. There were lots of skaters better than she was. Still, it didn't hurt to dream. You never knew. Stranger things had happened.

But even if she didn't come close to winning, just being in the Nationals was a dream come true. And she intended to enjoy every minute.

In the seats beside her, Tori's mother slept with her head on Roger Arnold's shoulder. Roger was Mrs. Carsen's boyfriend. Tori wished that her mother hadn't insisted that Roger come along. He was so annoying. Especially when he acted as if he and Tori were friends. How could she be friends with a boring grown-up like Roger? And when he tried to talk to Tori about her skating—what a joke! He didn't know anything about the sport.

Oh, well, Tori sighed inwardly. I've got to concentrate on my skating. I won't let anything else bother me. Especially not Roger. She would just pretend he wasn't there.

Nikki Simon and Alex Beekman, two other members of Silver Blades, sat in the seats behind Tori. Nikki was one of Tori's best friends, and Alex was Nikki's skating partner. Nikki had been a singles skater when she first joined Silver Blades two years before, but then she and Alex had teamed up. Nikki had been skating pairs ever since. She and Alex were skating in the Novice Pairs events at the Nationals.

Tori could hear Alex and Nikki talking quietly. "I heard that Carla Benson qualified for the Nationals, too," Alex said.

Carla Benson was a member of Blade Runners, another top skating club. She and Tori had been rivals for years.

"Carla's good, but I think Tori's even better," Nikki told Alex. "Wouldn't it be great if Tori beat her?"

Not *if*, thought Tori, *when*. No way would Carla beat her at the Nationals. That much she had promised herself.

Alex stood up and walked toward the back of the plane. Tori unfastened her seat belt and moved into his seat next to Nikki.

"I can't concentrate on this movie. I'm way too excited!" Tori exclaimed.

Nikki smiled, revealing her braces. Her green eyes flashed with excitement.

"Me too," Nikki agreed. "I still can't believe it. It all seems like a dream."

"I know. We've been imagining this for so long." Tori grinned. "One year, Jill and Dani and I played this game where we pretended we were all in the Nationals. One of us played the announcer, and the others were all skaters."

Nikki laughed. "Yeah. And I bet *you* always managed to take home the gold."

"Oh, no. We took turns!"

Since that time, Danielle Panati had dropped out of

Silver Blades. She had quit skating to concentrate on writing and working on the school newspaper.

Jill Wong had gone back to training at the well-known International Ice Academy in Denver. Tori, Jill, and Dani were still close friends. Tori patted the pocket that held her letter to Jill. She couldn't wait to write her friends about everything that happened this week.

Tori leaned closer to Nikki. "So how is Alex doing?" she asked. "He seems kind of down." Alex had broken up with his girlfriend just a few days before.

"He's taking it pretty hard, but he'll get over it," Nikki assured her. "Right now he needs to concentrate on skating, not romance."

"I'm sure Sarge will make sure that he does." Tori glanced across the aisle to where their two coaches were sitting. Kathy Bart was talking quietly to Dan Trapp.

Kathy was known as "Sarge" because she was so tough. Dan was completely different. Tori thought he acted like an annoying big brother. He was a big believer in positive thinking. He was always trying to get everyone to *think* their way into skating well. Plus he was always cheerful. He drove Tori crazy. But she had to admit that he had helped her skating.

I won't let Dan bother me this week, Tori vowed. There's too much at stake.

Tori glanced across the aisle and frowned. Amber Armstrong and her mother were sitting side by side.

Amber was watching Tori intently. Amber was the newest member of Silver Blades. Tori still couldn't believe that Amber had qualified as a Junior skater in the Nationals, too. She was only eleven! And though Tori had to admit that Amber was pretty good for her age, secretly she thought the judges also loved Amber because she was so small and cute.

Amber thought Dan was the greatest, and he obviously felt the same about her. Together, the two of them were more than Tori could take. And lately Amber had been trying to hang out with Tori all the time. Well, Tori didn't plan to spend this week baby-sitting an eleven-year-old. She wasn't going to let Amber— or anyone else—ruin her concentration. This was the Nationals! She was going there to skate her best. And that's what she intended to do.

Beside her, Nikki smiled and pointed to the seats in front of them. Tori's mother was still leaning her head against Roger's shoulder. "That's so cute," Nikki said.

"Cute?" Tori stared at Nikki. "You mean twisted, don't you?"

"Tori!" Nikki giggled.

"Really," Tori continued, "my mother is almost forty. But ever since she met Roger, she acts like she's fourteen!"

"Well, at least she's off your case," Nikki pointed out. "You should be glad that she's got someone else to worry about."

Mrs. Carsen was a former skater herself. She was

known for pushing Tori hard. But ever since Roger had come on the scene, she had lightened up. Everyone had noticed it. Lately she wasn't hanging around the rink nearly as much as she used to.

Mrs. Carsen worked as a clothing designer. That was how she had met Roger, who owned Arnold's department stores. She'd sold him some of her designs. Now she worked almost exclusively for him. She barely had time to make Tori's skating costumes anymore.

"You always wished your mom would ease up," Nikki told her. "Now she has."

"Yeah, I guess so," Tori admitted. The truth was, she was glad to have her mother off her back. But she wasn't sure she liked having to share her mother's attention.

And she was a little annoyed that Roger had come along on this trip. The old Corinne Carsen would have spent every minute of the competition with Tori. Now she would be dividing her time between Tori and Roger. It didn't seem fair—especially since this was the Nationals.

"They're announcing their engagement on Valentine's Day," Tori continued. "Can you believe how corny that is?"

"I think it's romantic," Nikki said.

"It might be romantic if it were Christopher Kane and Trisha McCoy," Tori said, referring to two of their favorite ice-skating champions. "Or maybe if Brad Pitt got together with Courteney Cox or something," Tori added. "But this is Mom and Roger we're talking about!"

"Well, I guess when it's your own mother, it's hard to see it that way, but—"

Before Nikki could finish, Amber shouted, "Look! There it is. There's San Jose."

"Ladies and gentlemen," the pilot announced, "we have begun our descent. We'll be landing at the San Jose airport in approximately fifteen minutes."

Tori grabbed Nikki's hand. "This is it. We're almost there!"

2

Dear Dani,

I can't believe I'm here at the Nationals and not competing. It's kind of weird. But it was really nice of my dad to treat me to this trip! He's got business in San Francisco, which isn't too far from San Jose. I'm meeting him there next week.

Thanks for all your advice, but I'm still worried that you-know-who will never be my valentine! Oh, well. I've got seven days to change his mind. Wish me luck!

Your lovesick friend,
Haley

"It's great that you could come, Haley." Dan Trapp hoisted Haley's suitcase off the sidewalk where the airport van had dropped her off. He led her into the hotel, smiling widely. "I know your being here means a lot to your teammates."

It was eight o'clock at night on the same day that the others had arrived in San Jose. Haley had flown out separately so that she wouldn't have to miss an extra day of school. Also, she didn't have to arrive early, like the others, to register for the competition.

Now, as Dan led her through the lobby of the hotel, she had mixed feelings. It was thrilling to be at the Nationals. But she felt some regret. She wished that she and Patrick had qualified. Patrick McGuire was her pairs partner. They were a perfectly matched team, and they had done well in the Regionals. But they had blown it in their long program at the Sectionals and had missed qualifying.

Well, she thought, for once I can really enjoy myself. She didn't have to worry about her skating; she could just have fun. The hotel was cool, she was in San Jose, and she intended to have a good time.

As she waited for an elevator, Nikki, Alex, and Tori burst out of the other one. Before Haley knew what was happening, they were hugging her. "We're all here. Can you believe it?" Nikki cried.

"It's so great you came, Haley. There's so much to see! There are some really incredible skaters competing," Tori said.

"We missed you on the flight out here. It was so boring! No one played any tricks on the flight attendants," Alex told her with a smile. Haley was known for her practical jokes.

"Well, don't worry. We've got seven whole days. And this place looks like it could use a little shaking up," Haley said, gazing around at the elegant hotel lobby.

"You're rooming with me." Nikki pulled Haley into the elevator. "Our room is so cool. Wait till you see it."

Nikki and Haley rode the elevator up to the eleventh floor. Nikki led the way down the hall to their room. "It's room eleven-oh-seven," she told Haley. "Doesn't that sound like a lucky number to you?"

"Definitely a good omen," Haley agreed. "Have you seen the rink yet?" she asked.

"Not yet," Nikki said, sliding her key into the lock. "We haven't had a chance. We spent hours at registration, and we just finished dinner." Nikki flung open the door to their room.

"Wow, this is incredible!" Haley gazed in surprise around the spacious room. There were two double beds, a small table and two chairs, a large chest of drawers, and a huge television. There was also a small refrigerator.

"Check out the bathroom," Nikki said.

"Cool! A phone! Just in case we want to call someone while we're brushing our teeth."

Haley dumped her stuff on the floor and collapsed onto the bed. She grabbed the remote control and flipped on the TV.

"A movie channel! I may be up all night. This is *so* cool. Our own room, with our own phone, TV, and refrigerator. This is going to be a blast," Haley cried.

"Yeah, but I do have to get plenty of sleep, don't forget," Nikki warned.

"Oh, I know," Haley assured her. "Don't worry. I won't forget why we're here."

Haley rolled over and watched Nikki as she finished unpacking her clothes. "So, how is everyone? Is Alex still unhappy?"

"He's better, I think. I hope now that we're here he'll forget all about Maria and concentrate on skating. I never thought they were right for each other, anyway," Nikki confided.

"Me either," Haley agreed. In fact, Alex had been so down for the last month that Haley had hoped he *would* break up with Maria.

Even though Alex was fifteen and two years ahead in school, he had begun talking to Haley a lot while he was going out with Maria. A few times he had really poured his heart out to her. He'd described all his feelings for Maria. Haley had found herself looking forward to their talks more and more . . . and wishing that Alex would notice her, too.

Haley thought it was great to be his friend. But it would be even better to be his girlfriend. If only they could talk about something besides Maria!

Haley hadn't told anyone except Danielle how she felt. She didn't want to tell Nikki yet. She wasn't sure how Nikki would feel. Nikki and Alex were partners, and Haley knew what that was like. Nikki was sort of possessive about Alex.

And now that they were at the Nationals, Nikki had made it clear that she wanted Alex to focus on skating and nothing else.

Nikki hung up her Silver Blades warm-up jacket. "On top of that, I was getting kind of sick of Alex's moping around all the time. He really let it affect his skating. When things were good between them, he skated well. But when they were bad, he skated badly."

"Alex is a pretty emotional guy," Haley commented.

"Yeah, but he's got to get some control. He can't let his emotions affect his performance." Nikki unpacked the last few items in her bag. She pointed to the bureau. "I left these extra drawers for you. Don't you want to put your stuff away?"

"Nah. I'll do it later. Right now I just want to enjoy being here." Haley lay back on the bed, clicking the remote. "Channel-surfing, my second-favorite sport!"

The phone rang and Haley grabbed it. "Alex!" she cried when she heard his voice.

"Hey," he greeted her. "We're going over to check out the rink. Meet us in the lobby in five minutes. Tell Nikki to bring her skates."

"Great!" Haley hung up quickly. "Come on," she told Nikki. "Everyone's going to the rink. Alex says to bring your skates." Haley rummaged in her bags, knocking some of her clothes onto the floor. She and Nikki pulled out their leggings and sweatshirts and changed quickly.

The girls hurried down to the lobby to meet the others.

It was a short walk from the hotel to the ice arena. In just a few minutes Nikki, Haley, Tori, and Alex found themselves outside the biggest skating facility any of them had ever seen.

Alex yanked open the double doors and swept his arm in a wide gesture. "Welcome, ladies, to the 1996 National Figure-Skating Championships, live from San Jose, California," he cried, imitating a sports announcer. "In the next week you will witness the country's top skaters locked in brutal competition. Who will take home the gold? Will it be Tori Carsen, the incredible singles skater from Seneca Hills, Pennsylvania? Or will it be light and lovely Nikki Simon, who'd do anything to win, including torturing her poor partner, *me*—the fabulous Alex!" Everyone giggled wildly.

But once they had stepped inside, even Alex was quiet, awed by the beautiful arena.

"Wow! This place is super." Nikki gazed around the enormous lobby. Through the glass windows they could see an immense expanse of perfectly groomed ice.

A huge red, white, and blue banner was strung over-

head: WELCOME U.S. NATIONAL FIGURE-SKATING CHAM-
PIONS!

"Look at that ice! It's beautiful!" Tori exclaimed.

"Let's try it out," Alex said. "That's what we came
for."

"Are you sure it's okay?" Nikki asked. She frowned.
"We already registered for the competition. That
means no extra practices before our events."

"This isn't a *real* practice," Alex told her. "This is for
fun!"

In one corner of the lobby a man in a dark gray
uniform sat reading a newspaper. His walkie-talkie
squawked every few minutes. "There's someone. A
night watchman or something. Let's ask," Haley said.

"Good idea. Go on, Alex, ask him," Nikki prodded.

"Me? Why me? You ask him," Alex protested.

"I'll ask him," Haley volunteered. "He's not going to
arrest us for asking." She approached the man and
said, "Excuse me, sir."

He looked up. "Can I help you, miss?"

"We're here for the Nationals, and, um, we were
wondering—would it be all right if we checked out
the rink? Do you think anyone would mind?"

The guard peered at the plastic badges that they
wore. The badges identified them as skaters in the
competition. Haley's said she was an official guest.

"I'm new here, but I guess it's okay," he said. "No
one else is using the rink now. Go ahead. I'll be right
here if you need me."

"Thanks," Haley said. "Go ahead, you guys. Hit the ice."

They raced into the rink area and put on their skates. Alex and Nikki were first on the ice. Haley watched as they fell into step side by side—almost automatically, it seemed. They began to run through their short program.

Watching them, Haley felt a pang of jealousy. She wished Patrick were there and that the two of them were practicing their own program and getting ready for the competition. It felt strange to be watching from the sidelines.

Am I crazy? I still get to be with my best friends at a major competition, Haley told herself. And I get to have fun. No pressure, no anxiety, just a really good time. Maybe I'll even get a few tips. Then, next year, I'll make it to the Nationals, too.

Nikki and Alex finished their program. Alex skated over to Haley. He smiled at her, and she felt her heart do a little flip of happiness.

"Do you miss Patrick?" Alex asked.

"Kind of," she told him. "Part of me really wishes we were competing. But another part of me is glad I don't have the pressure. You know what I mean?"

"Do I ever! Nikki's always so uptight before a competition," he said. Leaning closer, he whispered, "Will you do me a favor? Try to get her to relax, okay?"

"I'll try, but I can't promise anything." Haley paused. "Hey, I've got an idea." She dug around in her bag for a minute. She pulled out a plastic tube that held a brush and comb set. The tube made a perfect microphone.

"Ladies and gentlemen," she called, "on the ice now is the amazing Tori Carsen!"

She introduced Tori and Nikki and Alex. Then Haley had them run through their programs while she announced each move.

Tori found an official's jacket on the bleachers. She draped it over her shoulders and borrowed Haley's microphone. "It gives me great pleasure to announce the winner of the novice pairs event!" Tori held out an arm toward Nikki and Alex. "In an unbelievable upset victory, the gold medal goes to Nikki—"

Before she could finish, the doors to the rink slammed open. A large gray-haired man with an angry red face appeared. He was yelling at the night watchman, who followed sheepishly along behind him. Nikki and Alex froze in the middle of the rink.

"How could you let those kids out on the ice?" the gray-haired man ranted.

Nikki and Alex joined Tori and Haley at the barrier. "Is there a problem?" Haley asked.

"There certainly is," the gray-haired man told them. "This rink is closed." He reached into his pocket and whipped out a notepad. "Give me your names."

"But we weren't practicing," Alex protested. "We're sorry if we weren't supposed to be skating yet, but—"

"You're skating in the competition?" The man peered at Alex's badge.

"Yes, sir," Alex said. "For Silver Blades, from Seneca Hills, Pennsylvania."

Haley winced. She wished Alex hadn't said that. They could be in big trouble.

"We're really sorry," Tori apologized.

The man stared at her. "Where did you find that jacket? It's only for judges."

Tori gulped. "Are you a judge?"

"I am. Now take those skates off—and that jacket— and leave the rink. You'll have time to practice during regular hours tomorrow."

Tori quietly slipped off the official's jacket. The judge reached out to take it from her.

The three of them quickly took off their skates. The judge watched them impatiently and waited while they left the rink. The doors clanged shut behind them.

No one said a word until they were several yards away from the arena. Then Tori burst out angrily, "What an old grouch! It's not like we were trying to make trouble."

"But he's a *judge*," Nikki said. "What if he holds this against us? What if it ruins our chances at a good score?"

"We'll be judged on our skating ability and nothing else. He won't hold this against us," Alex insisted.

"I hope not!" Nikki seemed very upset.

"Well, we'll just have to prove that we're winners. Next time he runs into us, he'll see some great skating," Tori declared.

For a moment everyone was silent.

"Well, I thought it was kind of funny," Haley finally said. "I thought Tori looked like she was going to faint when he caught her wearing his jacket!"

Tori and Alex burst out laughing. Haley noticed that Nikki didn't crack a smile.

"Hey, it's okay. No harm done," Haley said.

Tori threw her arm around Nikki's shoulder. "Don't worry. It'll be okay."

"Let's hope so," Nikki mumbled.

Alex met Haley's eyes. "See what I mean?" he whispered. "The pressure is on. I'm counting on you to help Nikki ease up."

"No problem," Haley assured him. Alex could definitely count on her. She'd never let him down!

3

Dear Amber,
  I'm so proud of you! You're really on your way to the top! And look how grown-up you've become! Good luck, and keep up the hard work.

                                              Love,
                                              Dad

Early the next morning Amber and her mother stood in the lobby of the ice arena. They gazed through the windows at the empty rink.

"Great! We're here in plenty of time," Amber said.

"It is a fabulous rink, isn't it?" Her mother stifled a yawn and smiled at Amber. "Well, what are you waiting for? Do your off-ice warm-up."

Amber was glad she had made her mother wake up

extra early so they could get to the rink as soon as it opened.

Amber had been really nervous ever since they arrived in San Jose. She was the youngest junior ladies' skater in the whole competition. Everyone seemed so much cooler than she was. And lately, she hadn't been skating her best.

As she started stretching Amber felt her muscles begin to relax. She rolled her neck and shoulders up and down several times. She twisted from side to side. She put each leg up on the barrier and stretched, leaning as far over as she could go. She felt her hamstrings loosen. She tried several jumps in place, trying to get the most height each time.

Soon the rink would be packed with skaters and judges and spectators. Anxiety levels would be high. And Amber was already feeling anxious.

Amber noticed that several other skaters were getting ready to go on the ice. Nikki, Alex, and Tori had arrived, too. They were lacing up their skates. Amber hurried over to where her mother stood behind the barrier.

"Good luck, honey," her mother said. She reached down and gave Amber a hug and a loud kiss. Amber drew away.

"Mom! Not in front of everyone!" she cried. "You don't need to treat me like a little kid." Couldn't her mom understand? She was growing up. She was part of the Silver Blades team now, skating as a junior lady in the Nationals. The last thing she wanted was to be treated like a baby. Her dad seemed to realize that. Why couldn't her mom?

Amber noticed her mother's hurt look. She knew she shouldn't be so mean. After all, both her parents had scrimped and saved to come up with the money to send her to San Jose. Amber's skating meant a big sacrifice for them.

But she just couldn't stand it when her mother treated her like a baby. How would she ever get to be better friends with Tori, Haley, and Nikki if they thought of her as a little kid?

Amber removed her skate guards and glided quickly over to Dan. He was waiting for her on the ice by the barrier. Kathy was Amber's official coach, but that morning Dan was going to be working with Amber so that Kathy could work with Nikki and Alex.

"You look fantastic, kiddo," Dan told her. "Keep your concentration and you'll be terrific tomorrow."

Amber was scheduled to skate her short program the very next morning. She had less time to prepare than Tori, who wouldn't skate until the day after that. Dan's extra attention helped calm her nerves.

Meanwhile, she tried to feel the warm glow that Dan's praise always gave her. He always knew just what to say.

Tori skated over to them. "Isn't it time to get started, Dan?"

"Soon." Dan smiled at Tori. "When you get out on

the ice, relax and try to get the feel of this new rink,"
he suggested. "You seem tense, Tori. Take it easy for
the first few minutes. You'll feel better," Dan told her.

"I'll still be tense," Tori snapped. "I'm about to skate
in the biggest event of my life!"

"Forget about the event. Focus on your skating and
your teammates," Dan advised. "We're all here for
you, and we know you can do a great job."

"I'd be a lot less tense if we could cut this feel-good
stuff and get to work. We don't have that much practice time," Tori complained.

Amber bit her lip. Tori always seemed so annoyed
with Dan. But Amber thought Dan was right. It *was*
relaxing, focusing on her skating instead of the event.
And following Dan's advice usually made her feel a
part of the Silver Blades team.

Amber glanced at Tori with admiration. She looked
fantastic in another new outfit—a purple dress with
turquoise stripes down the sides, purple tights, and
turquoise gloves. The colors brought out the blue of
her eyes and set off her blond curls. You couldn't help
noticing Tori on the ice. In fact, it was hard to take
your eyes off her.

Amber gazed down at her own outfit. Next to Tori
she looked really boring. She was only wearing a pair
of black leggings and a white sweatshirt. She had to
save her good skating dress for the competition. Tori
was lucky—she had more outfits than anyone else.
And they were all beautiful.

Dan told them which moves to practice. Then an announcer called the official beginning of practice. The skaters charged the ice for their first practice session of the morning.

The time flew by. Amber tried to feel confident as she was skating. She made herself forget about everything but her jumps, spins, and footwork. Still, she was more nervous than usual. She wobbled on her double flip.

At a few minutes before eleven Dan said, "Okay, girls, that was a good workout! I think you've earned your lunch. Don't forget today is the big barbecue. Take some time to relax, and I'll see you outside."

Amber gazed up at the bleachers. Her mother was waving frantically and signaling to her. Now what? Amber thought. She hoped her mother didn't expect to eat lunch with her. She wanted to eat with Tori and the other kids. She pretended she hadn't seen her mother waving. Instead, she glanced at Tori, who was still working on a sit spin.

Amber decided to try her double flip again. She was determined not to leave the ice until Tori did. She prepared to go into the jump, hoping her mother would take the hint and go to lunch on her own.

Tori finished working and skated off the ice. Amber hurried after her.

"I'm starving! Are you?" Amber began, trying to start a conversation.

"I guess so." Tori shrugged.

As Amber and Tori stepped off the ice, a tall girl with long blond hair approached.

"Well, well," the girl said, "look who's here. Tori Carsen! I was wondering if any of you Silver Blades skaters would make it to the Nationals."

"Hi, Carla," Tori muttered.

Amber knew that Tori wasn't too happy to see Carla Benson. They always gave each other a hard time.

"So, who else is here from Silver Blades?" Carla asked.

"Nikki and Alex are skating pairs," Tori answered. "And Haley's here, but she's not competing."

"What about Jill Wong? Oh, that's right. She didn't make it to the Regionals or Sectionals. She skates for the Ice Academy now, anyway. It must have been tough for Silver Blades to lose their best skater," Carla said with mock sympathy.

Amber saw Tori's face turn red. Amber stepped closer to Carla. "We're all really happy for Jill. And besides, we've got *plenty* of good skaters left. Like Tori." Amber glared at Carla.

"Of course," Carla said. "I know how good Tori is. I just think I'll be skating my best this week. Maybe I'll even be the best one here."

"Don't be so sure," Tori whispered quietly, so that only Amber could hear. She sat down on the bench to take off her skates. Amber immediately sat next to her.

"And who's this? Your little sister?" Carla asked sarcastically.

Amber felt her cheeks flush.

"This is Amber Armstrong, our newest Silver Blades member." Tori turned to Amber. "This is Carla Benson. She skates with the Blade Runners from Vermont."

"Hi, Carla," Amber said, trying not to giggle. Tori and Carla were acting so polite. Everyone knew they couldn't stand each other.

"Well, hi there!" Carla grinned at Amber. "You sure are cute. How old are you?"

Amber glared back at her. Cute? Ooohh! Just who does she think she is? "I'm eleven," Amber said, trying to sound dignified.

"Only eleven. You must be scared, competing against more experienced skaters," Carla said.

"Just wait till you see her skate, Carla," Tori boasted. "Then you'll know why we wanted her in Silver Blades. Right, Amber?"

Amber nodded happily. Tori had stuck up for her!

"Well, I'll be watching you, Amber." Carla stepped onto the ice and glided into a series of graceful crossovers.

"I can't stand that stupid Carla!" Tori said, yanking off her right skate. "If I don't beat her, I'll die. I'll absolutely die."

"You will beat her, Tori. I know you will." Amber hurried to change the subject. "And now I'm *really* starved, aren't you? I hope there's tons of food at this barbecue."

But Tori wasn't paying attention to her. She was watching Carla with an intense look of determination. "I am definitely going to beat her," Tori muttered.

Carla stepped into a flashy spin. She's good, Amber thought, but she's not *that* good. I am *not* going to let her scare me. Tori thinks she can beat Carla. Well, I can beat Carla, too!

4

Amber tore her gaze away from Carla. Next to her, Tori jammed her skates into her bag and stood up.

"Tori, I'm almost ready. Wait for me," Amber said.

Tori frowned. "Don't you have to eat with your mother or something?" she asked.

"No. I'm going to eat with you. I don't have to stay with my mother all the time."

"Okay, but hurry it up." Tori seemed annoyed.

Amber quickly crammed her feet into her beat-up sneakers and grabbed her skating bag. Tori headed toward the lobby.

Does Tori like me or not? Amber wondered. Why would she stick up for me to Carla if she doesn't like me? And why can't she slow down a little? Amber struggled to keep up with Tori. She followed her closely through the crowd that filled the grassy area behind the rink.

"Tori, Amber, over here!" Haley called to them. She was standing with Nikki and Alex. "There you are! I've been looking for you guys. Let's get in line."

"Yeah. I'm starved, and it smells great," Alex agreed.

There were several buffet tables. The skaters and their guests crowded into lines in front of them. Amber followed the others to what looked like the shortest line.

Tori turned to Nikki, Haley, and Alex. "Guess who I saw."

"Nancy Kerrigan?" Haley said. "I heard that she's going to be here."

"No, Carla Benson," Tori announced. "And she's more obnoxious than ever."

"Yeah, she's a real pain," Amber piped up. "She started making these nasty cracks about—" Amber was about to explain to them how Tori had stuck up for her. But Tori cut her off before she could finish.

"I have to beat Carla. I just have to!" Tori exclaimed.

"Remember that time in Lake Placid when she was so sure she'd win?" Nikki asked.

Tori groaned. "Do I!" She and the others began talking about people and places that Amber had never heard of. Amber followed them to the line in silence.

They were almost up to where the food was being

served. Amber grabbed a plate and silverware. Lunch looked delicious. There were barbecued chicken and ribs, and a big selection of salads, fruits, and rolls.

Suddenly she saw Tori nudge Nikki and whisper, "Do you see what I see?" Tori was staring at a cute boy just ahead of them in line.

"Shhh," Nikki whispered. "He'll hear you."

"Do you know who he is?" Tori asked.

Nikki shook her head.

The boy piled his plate high with food. "He seems to have a healthy appetite," Nikki joked.

"I've got to find out who he is. He's incredible-looking," Tori said.

Amber watched as the boy made his way through the line. He was probably about fifteen or sixteen. He had straight dark hair, worn longer on one side. His flannel shirt was open over a black T-shirt. Tori stared after him as he took his plate and disappeared into the crowd.

"Haley, Alex, do you know who that was?" Tori asked.

"Who was who?" Alex grinned.

"The boy in front of you in line! I've got to find out his name," Tori said.

"Never saw him before. Sorry," Alex replied.

"Me neither," Haley said. "But I'll keep my ears open. Maybe we can find out."

They spotted an empty table. All five of them hurried to sit. This is so cool, Amber thought. She was glad she had ditched her mother to have lunch with the older kids.

"Have you seen all the reporters and photographers around here?" Tori asked. "One of us might get an interview. I hope it's me."

"I don't know if I *want* to be interviewed. It might make me too nervous," Nikki admitted.

"Not me. I think it would be cool," Tori said. "My mom designs my outfits especially so I *will* get noticed. And so I'll really stand out when I'm on the ice." She paused, took a bite of chicken, and then went on.

"Of course, I haven't totally decided which dress to wear for the short program and the long program. I have five to choose from," she continued. "Mom said we should decide after we've seen what the lighting is like here. It can really make a difference on camera."

"Really?" Amber asked.

Amber knew that some of the events would be taped and that the winners would probably be shown on television each day. So it was important to look good when you competed.

Tori glanced at Amber. "What are you planning to wear?"

Amber thought about the peach-colored skating dress that she and her mom had bought. She had been happy when they first found it. There had also been an unusual black and white dress that Amber had loved. But her mom had felt it was too sophisticated, and anyway, it was way too expensive. They'd settled for the peach. But when Amber thought about it now, it seemed kind of babyish.

"I've seen Amber's dress," Haley said. "It's cool."

Amber smiled gratefully at Haley for trying to make her feel better. But if only her mother had let her get that black and white dress!

"I, uh, thought I'd wear the same dress for both events," Amber said, "because I really like it a lot." She didn't want Tori to know that she owned only one good dress.

"Enough!" Alex interrupted. "I really wish Patrick were here. Then we could talk about something besides skating dresses."

The others laughed. "Poor Alex. You *are* kind of outnumbered," Haley said. "Come on. Let's hit the dessert table."

As they were finishing dessert Tori said, "I wonder if we could watch Carla's practice later. I'd love to see how strong she looks."

"Good idea. We might as well stick around the rink," Nikki said.

"Yeah. There's nothing to do back at the hotel," Amber agreed.

Amber swallowed the last of her cake. She glanced up and saw her mother hurrying toward her.

"Amber, honey, I've been looking all over for you! Did you get your lunch?" Mrs. Armstrong called out.

"Yes, Mom," Amber said. She was so embarrassed! No one else's parents were checking on them every five minutes.

"Well, good. I think it's time we got back to the hotel. I'd like you to rest this afternoon. You have a busy schedule for the next few days."

"I don't need to rest, Mom. I'm fine," Amber said through clenched teeth.

"Well, *I* need to rest. And I'd like you to come with me," her mother replied.

"But everyone else is staying. Why can't I stay with them?" Amber knew she was whining, but she couldn't stop herself.

"Amber, I want you to come back to the hotel with me. *Now,*" her mother added firmly.

Amber knew there was no point in arguing. The others probably thought she was a baby already, being dragged home by her mother like a two-year-old. She followed her mother away from the arena.

"Bye, Tori. Bye, guys," she called.

"Wasn't that a delicious lunch?" her mother asked. Amber was too angry to answer. They returned to the hotel in silence.

Back in the room, Amber pulled her peach outfit from the closet. Maybe there was some way to fix it, to make it look more grown-up.

"I'm going to try this on," she told her mother. "Just to make sure it still fits and all."

"Still fits!" her mother exclaimed. "I certainly hope so. We just bought it two weeks ago."

"I know. But I want to see how it looks."

Amber pulled on the dress and a pair of flesh-colored tights. She gazed at her reflection in the full-length mirror on the back of the closet door.

The dress was a pretty color. But how would it look on TV? Tori had said some colors looked different on camera.

And what was she going to do with her hair? She couldn't just let it hang there. Suddenly she thought it looked awful. *She* looked awful. Like a little kid.

"What am I going to do with my hair, Mom? It looks gross!" Amber cried.

"Your hair?" Her mother glanced up from the desk, where she was writing a letter. "Your hair is lovely, honey. We'll put it back like we always do. We have that pretty peach ribbon to go with your dress, remember?"

"It looks stupid. I should get my hair cut or something. And everyone else is wearing a different dress for their long and short programs. I'm the only one who's wearing the same dress for both events." Amber pouted.

"I'm sorry. But you know how tight money is. And the peach dress is so flattering."

"Tori brought five different dresses. And they're all great," Amber cried. "Couldn't we get just one more dress?"

Her mother frowned. "We've already spent so much on your new outfit and on the flight out here. We're way behind. I just don't think we can. I'm afraid you'll have to make do."

As Amber gazed in the mirror she felt worse and worse. Tori's words kept coming back to her: "What are you planning to wear?" Maybe Tori was afraid Amber would look awful—and embarrass everyone in Silver Blades!

Amber peeled off her outfit and crammed it into the closet. She flung herself onto the bed and stared at the ceiling.

Her mother came to sit beside her. "Honey, what's wrong? It's not like you to be so upset over a skating outfit. Is there something you're not telling me?"

Amber turned her face away, wishing her mother would just leave her alone. How could she possibly explain? Her mother would never understand. Tears welled up in her eyes.

"Sweetie, what is it?" her mother asked again. Amber could hear the concern in her voice, and before she knew it, she had burst out crying.

"It's just that . . . that I'm sick of being treated like a baby! I'm only three years younger than Tori. But everyone treats me like a little kid. And it's your fault! You act like I can't do anything for myself!"

"I don't," her mother said. "Besides, the others *are* older than you. You can't expect them to treat you as if you were the same age."

"Well, I don't want to be treated like a baby, either. And my outfit makes me look like a baby. Tori has all her outfits designed to show up against the ice. But mine will look horrible. I just know it."

"Amber, I hope people will be watching your skating, not your outfit. This isn't a fashion show. It's the U.S. National Figure-Skating Championships. You're here because you're a wonderful skater," her mother declared. "You should be proud of yourself. Why be in such a hurry to grow up? You're doing just fine."

Amber groaned. Her mother was right in one way. She did want people to pay attention to her skating, not her outfit. But she wished that just this once she could have the perfect dress. Like Tori.

"I think this is partly nerves," her mother said. "You really should try to rest for a while."

"Okay, Mom." Amber lay back on the bed. She was too tired to argue anymore. She closed her eyes, but in a minute they popped open again.

Across the room she saw her mother take out her wallet and count their money. A look of concern crossed her face.

Amber thought of the hours her mother put in at her job, taking on extra typing on top of her regular secretarial work. And she thought of all the things her mother had done without to pay for Amber's skating lessons—and for this trip.

Suddenly she really felt bad. She shouldn't have complained about the new outfit.

"Mom," she announced, "forget what I said. You're right. It's the skating that counts. Not the dress."

Her mother smiled. "Good for you! That's the right spirit!"

Yeah, Amber thought. If only I really meant it.

5

Dear Jill,

There are a lot of fantastic skaters here. It's kind of scary, but I'm feeling tough! Good thing for me that you're not here! (Just kidding.) I really hope I place in the top ten. I'm pretty sure I'll do better than Amber. I only wish I felt stronger than Carla Benson. I watched her practice yesterday, and I hate to say it, but she's looking good.

How's everything at the Academy? We miss you!

Love,
Tori

P.S. Possible valentine sighting! There are lots of really cute guys here. I have my eye on a special one. Who knows?

Almost everyone had gone back to the hotel to change. There was a big opening-night banquet later. But Tori had stayed behind. She wanted to run through her short program one more time, even if she had to do it off the ice. After all, she'd be performing it the day after next. And it had to be perfect.

Back at home, Tori had thought her program was solid. But since they had been at the Nationals, she felt that it wasn't as good as it should be. In just one day of practice she had seen many terrific skaters. She realized that she couldn't measure up to a lot of them. Still, Tori was used to being among the best. And she was willing to work hard to be number one.

She pulled her headphones over her ears and turned up the volume of her Walkman. Her skating music began. Tori walked to the end of the hallway, where it opened into the rink.

In her sneakers, she leaped up and performed a flying camel, and then dropped into an imitation of a sit spin. Even in sneakers, she could practice the intricate footwork pattern that Blake Michaels, the Silver Blades choreographer, had worked out especially for her. She kept her head high, facing an imaginary audience, as Blake had taught her. The stands were empty now, but on the opening day of the competition they would be packed.

Tori gazed out into the stands. One person lingered

there, watching her. Tori gasped. It was the cute boy she had noticed at lunch! He was alone, and he was staring at her intently.

Tori felt a thrill run through her, but she pretended not to notice him. She spun around in the hallway and tried to focus on her routine again. She finished her program with a spectacular series of jumps. As she stood holding her final position she felt really good. She glanced at the stands again. The boy was gone!

She sighed and sat down on a bench to take off her Walkman. It was late. She'd have to race back to the hotel to get changed in time. She had promised her mom and Roger that she would meet them before the banquet. They would be wondering where she was.

As she put her Walkman in her skate bag, she noticed that her skate laces were beginning to fray. She would have to get some new ones the next morning. Tori lifted the bag and was getting ready to go when she sensed someone approach. She glanced up. The boy was only a few feet away. He wasn't wearing skating clothes, and Tori hadn't seen him on the ice. What was he doing there?

"I watched you skate earlier," he said suddenly. "You're good."

"Thanks," Tori replied. "Are you a skater?"

"Nope. But I know good skating when I see it." He grinned.

Tori knew she was staring at him but she couldn't

help it. He was so good-looking. I've got to say something, she thought. But all she could think about was how cute he was.

"My name's Pierce, by the way. Pierce Lawrence."

"I'm Tori Carsen."

"From Pennsylvania, right? Silver Blades?" Pierce asked.

"Right, but how'd you know?" Tori couldn't hide her surprise.

"I have my methods," he said with another grin.

Tori pretended to concentrate on packing her skate bag. "So, what are you doing here? If you're not a skater, I mean," she added.

"I'm here with my family. I go to boarding school back East, but we're on midsemester break," he explained.

"Oh. You're in high school?" Tori asked. What a stupid question, she thought. Obviously he was in high school. She could tell that he was older than she was.

"Tenth grade," Pierce said.

Tori gulped. She had to change the subject before Pierce asked what grade she was in. She wanted him to think she was older than an eighth-grader! She glanced at her watch. "Wow, it's getting late. I've got to hurry. Are you going to the banquet tonight?"

"Yeah, I'll be there with my parents. My dad is a judge. I figured this whole competition thing would be one big snooze, but now that I've met you, I'm thinking it won't be so bad." He flashed an incredible smile.

Tori could feel her heart pounding. She could hardly take her eyes off him. She hoped he couldn't tell how flustered she was. She stood up. "Well, I've got to get back to the hotel. Maybe I'll see you later."

"Definitely. I'll look for you," Pierce promised. "In fact, I won't eat a bite until I find you!"

Tori grabbed her skating bag and hurried toward the exit. He really must like her! Suddenly she couldn't wait to get to the banquet.

She raced back to the hotel to tell Nikki and Haley all about Pierce. As she crossed the lobby she heard her friends calling her. They were already changed and ready for the banquet.

"Tori, where've you been? It's almost time for dinner," Nikki said.

"I know. I wanted to run through my program one more time. And then I met that cute guy from lunch!"

"Really? Is he a skater?" Haley asked.

"No, but his father's a judge! Can you believe it? And he wants to meet me at the banquet tonight. I've got to get dressed!" Tori exclaimed. She headed toward the elevators.

"That's so cool. You're going to have a valentine after all," Haley teased.

Nikki didn't say anything.

"What's wrong, Nikki?" Tori asked. "Don't you think it's cool?"

Nikki shrugged. "I don't know. It doesn't seem like the time to think about romance. I want to concentrate on skating while I'm here, and nothing else."

"Well, when you get a look at Pierce again, you might change your mind," Tori said with a smile. "He's incredible."

Up in her room, Tori found a note from her mother. "Tori dear, Roger and I are going to take a walk before dinner. We'll meet you at the banquet. Love, Mom."

Tori crumpled the note and tossed it into the trash. No problem, she thought. That would make it easier to find Pierce.

Tori showered and dressed in a new pair of navy blue silk pants with a matching vest over a white blouse. She checked her appearance in the mirror. She had to admit she looked good. And definitely older than eighth grade.

As soon as she entered the banquet hall, she spotted Pierce. He was standing close to the door. When he noticed her, he waved and hurried toward her.

"Hey, there you are. This is a total bore. But now that you're here, things are looking up," he greeted her. He had changed into black jeans with a gray shirt and a matching gray and white patterned tie. With his dark eyes and hair, Tori thought he looked even more handsome than before.

"Have you eaten yet?" Tori asked him.

"Of course not. I've been waiting for you. But we'd better hurry. These skaters don't waste any time,"

Pierce said as they passed a group with plates piled high. "See what I mean? Come on, let's get in line."

He put an arm around her waist and steered her toward the buffet. Tori couldn't believe how smooth he was. He was so unlike any of the guys she hung out with at home.

When they had filled their plates with food, Pierce led her to a table for two in the back of the room.

"Is this okay? I'm trying to avoid my father's table. I'd much rather eat alone with you."

"This is fine," Tori assured him.

As soon as they sat down Pierce started asking all about her. How long had she been skating? How did she manage with school and everything? He really seemed interested in her answers.

She had never met a guy who wanted to know so much about her. She found herself telling him about her mother and Roger, and how they were getting engaged on Valentine's Day.

"What about you?" she said finally. "I've been doing all the talking. Now it's your turn. Tell me about boarding school. Is it horrible, or do you like it?"

Pierce shrugged. "I guess it's okay. Some of the kids are cool. But there are an awful lot of rules. I'm not big on rules. Of course, anything's better than living at home. My dad is on my case from morning till night."

"Your dad the judge?" Tori asked.

Pierce nodded. "He can't understand that not everyone is like him. When he's not judging skating events, he's a surgeon, specializing in sports injuries—Dr. Pierce Lawrence, Sr. He's also involved with about fifteen major companies. And he heads up all these cultural committees in his spare time. I have an older brother who's in medical school and who is also the ninth-ranked amateur tennis player. No one can figure me out." Pierce smiled.

Tori nodded, not really knowing what to make of it. "What do you like to do?"

Pierce shrugged. "Party. What else is there?"

She laughed. "But you must have some interests."

"The way I see it, you're only a teenager once. There'll be plenty of time to grind it out later. For now, I plan to enjoy myself. Know what I mean?"

"Sure," Tori said. Does he really mean that, or is he just trying to impress me? she wondered. It would be fun to find out.

When they finished dinner, Pierce took her hand and led her through the crowd to his parents' table. Tori was nervous at the thought of meeting them. What would they be like? she wondered. She especially wanted to make a good impression on his father, since he was a judge.

"There you are, darling! I was just asking your father if he had seen you. And who's your little friend? Isn't she cute!" A pretty woman in a black satin pantsuit held out her hand to Tori. "I'm Lucille Lawrence."

"Tori, this is my mother. Mom, this is Tori Carsen. She's a skater from Pennsylvania."

"Oh, you must sit down and tell me about yourself," Mrs. Lawrence cried. "I'm absolutely in awe of you young athletes. When I think of the discipline—"

"Tori, I'm going to get a Coke. Want anything?" Pierce asked her.

"No, thanks," Tori said politely, wishing he wouldn't leave her alone with his mother.

"I'm so glad Pierce has found a friend," his mother went on. "I was worried that he'd be bored to tears. Now, tell me . . ." Mrs. Lawrence began to ask Tori endless questions about her skating. Finally she said, "Oh, there's my husband. And here's Pierce junior coming back with his Coke."

Mrs. Lawrence signaled to her husband. Tori glanced at him—and wished she could sink beneath the table and crawl out the other side. It was the judge who had caught them at the rink the night before.

Please don't let him recognize me, Tori prayed. She could feel the blood rushing to her face as Mrs. Lawrence introduced them.

"Tori Carsen. Haven't I seen you skate?" Dr. Lawrence asked.

"Well, I'm from Pennsylvania," Tori said, trying to be vague.

"And what club are you with?"

"Um, Silver Blades," she mumbled.

"What was that?"

Tori took a deep breath.

"Silver Blades," she said a bit louder.

All of a sudden his smile faded. He glanced at his son with a frown. "Yes, Silver Blades. Why am I not surprised that you would end up with my son?"

Pierce looked confused by his father's remark. Tori couldn't think of anything to say. She wished she could run. Finally Mrs. Lawrence spoke. "Well, I know these skaters have to get a good night's sleep. It's time we let them go home, right, Tori?"

Before Tori could answer, Pierce said, "I'm going to stay here awhile. I'll meet you back in the room later, Dad."

Pierce grabbed Tori's hand and pulled her away from the table. "Let's get out of here and take a walk or something. Okay?" he asked.

"I don't know. . . . I told my mom I would meet her here," Tori answered. "I really should try to find her. And my friends, too."

"You can see them anytime. You and I should concentrate on getting to know each other. What do you say?" Pierce smiled down at her.

Tori's heart thumped wildly inside her chest. How could she say no?

"Well, I probably shouldn't leave the hotel," Tori told him. "I haven't even seen my mom yet tonight."

"There's a terrace off the lobby. We could go out

there and talk for a while," he suggested. "It's still pretty early. And it's a really nice night."

Tori checked her watch. It was five minutes to ten, and ten was her curfew, but she *would* be in the hotel. What would it hurt if she was a few minutes late getting back to her room?

"Sure. That sounds good," she said.

They left the banquet room and walked through the hotel.

"So you've met my father," Pierce said.

"Well, you could say that." Tori told him about the night before and how his father had caught them on the ice. When Pierce heard that Tori had been wearing an official's jacket, he burst out laughing. "I wish I could have been there. I'd have loved to see the look on his face. I bet he was furious."

"I think he was pretty mad," Tori agreed. "But we really didn't mean any harm by it. We thought it would be okay to skate."

Pierce shook his head. "That's the way my dad is. He thinks all kids are out for trouble. You weren't hurting anything by skating. But you didn't have his permission, so in his mind it was a big deal."

"I just hope it doesn't influence his decisions," Tori said.

"To be honest, I don't think it will. One thing about my father, he's fair about stuff like that. He might hate you, but if you skate a clean program, he'll admit it.

He'll judge you on your skating, nothing else," Pierce told her.

They came to a set of glass doors. Pierce held them open, and Tori stepped onto a lovely terrace.

Moonlight spilled over them. Tori could hardly believe her luck. She was in California, about to skate in the Nationals, and she was standing in the moonlight with the most incredible-looking guy she'd ever met.

Was this a dream? Must be, she decided. Because it was definitely too good to be true.

6

Dear Amber,
  Keep your heart set on your goal!

Amber felt the note in her pocket. It had come in the hotel mail the previous afternoon. She didn't know who had sent it, but it made her feel really good. She had decided she would keep it with her all week, kind of like a good-luck charm.

"Well, this is it. The big day." Amber's mother beamed at her across the table.

They were sitting in the hotel coffee shop eating breakfast. At least Amber was eating breakfast. Her mother was drinking coffee. She said she wasn't hungry, but Amber had a feeling she didn't want to spend any money.

Amber didn't feel like eating too much herself because of the butterflies in her stomach. But she knew
she had to eat something. She needed to keep up her
strength. In less than an hour she'd be skating her
short program.

I'm skating in the Nationals today! Today's the day
I'm skating in the Nationals. She kept repeating it to
herself, over and over. She still couldn't believe it.

"You're awfully quiet this morning. Nerves?" her
mother asked.

"Yeah," Amber admitted. "But I'm ready. I know I
am."

"Of course you are. You looked great on the ice yesterday," her mother told her. "Still, it's only natural to
be nervous. Who wouldn't be?"

Amber nodded. She spread cream cheese on her bagel and took a bite. It tasted like cardboard, but she
forced herself to eat it anyway.

The waitress stopped by their booth. "How is everything?" she asked. She raised her coffeepot. "Would
you like more coffee?" she asked.

"Oh, I don't think—," Amber's mother started to
say.

"Free refills," the waitress added. "What can you
lose, right?"

"Okay. And then we'd like the check, please," Mrs.
Armstrong said.

As the waitress wrote up their check, she glanced

at Amber's Silver Blades warm-up jacket. "Are you skating today? You look awfully young."

"She'll be skating her short program in the junior ladies' competition," Mrs. Armstrong announced proudly. "I'm so glad she gets to skate on the first day. Half of the girls won't skate their short programs until tomorrow. I don't think I could wait that long. I'm too nervous already!"

"Oh, my! How exciting!" The waitress smiled at Amber. "Tell me your name. I'll keep my fingers crossed for you," she promised.

"Amber Armstrong," Amber told her, pleased at the attention.

"Well, good luck to you, Amber. I'll be rooting for you!" The waitress moved on to the next table.

Amber finished her bagel. "Ready," she announced.

"Before we go to the rink, I have something to show you. It's back in the room," her mother told her.

In their room upstairs, Mrs. Armstrong hurried to the closet. "Ready in a minute," she called. She seemed excited about something. "Close your eyes!"

Amber closed her eyes. It sounded as though her mother was lifting something out of the closet. Had her mother fixed up the peach skating dress? Amber wondered. But how could she have done that?

"Okay. You can look now," her mother announced. "Surprise!"

Amber opened her eyes. Her mother was holding a

skating dress. But it wasn't the peach one. It was a brand-new dress! As Amber stared, her heart sank. The new outfit was baby blue, but it looked exactly like the peach dress. Only this one was trimmed with a giant bow at the neck. It was *so* babyish—worse than the peach.

Her mother held out the new outfit proudly. A big smile spread across her face.

"I got to thinking," her mother explained. "You were so upset the other day. Maybe you *do* need two dresses. I found this one in the Pro Shop at the rink. I sneaked over there yesterday afternoon while you were practicing. Isn't it darling?"

Amber felt like crying. Her mother was thrilled with her surprise, but Amber couldn't bring herself to tell her she didn't like it.

"What's wrong, Amber? Aren't you excited?"

"Sure . . . I really like it. It's just that I thought we couldn't afford a new dress. Maybe you should take it back," she suggested.

"Now, don't you start worrying about money," her mother said. "That's my business. You just worry about doing your best out there on the ice."

Amber took the dress and tried to smile.

"It's great, Mom. Really. Thanks," she said, giving her mother a hug. She knew that her mother would have to scrimp to make up for the money she'd spent on the dress. Already that morning her mom had refused the second cup of coffee at breakfast—before she knew it was free. Amber couldn't tell her mom how she really felt.

Amber pulled the dress on, forcing herself to look happy. She could barely stand to face the mirror.

"You look great," her mom cried. "Now let's get over to the rink!"

"Twenty minutes until your short program, Amber," Dan said. "Kathy will be here soon. But first I want to say a few things." He put both hands on her shoulders. "You ready? You feeling good?"

Amber nodded. "I think so. My stomach feels like there's a marching band inside it. But I think I'm ready."

Dan squatted down so that his face was level with hers. "Listen to me. You are ready," he said slowly, emphasizing each word with a squeeze of her shoulders. "I know it. I watch you every day, and I've rarely seen anyone as ready as you are. So I'm not worried. I'm just going to sit here and enjoy myself. I know I'll be watching some of the best skating I'll ever see." He smiled. "So you tell that marching band to start playing a victory march. Now go out there and enjoy yourself."

Amber felt her stomach ease up a bit. Dan was right. She was as ready as she'd ever be.

Suddenly Kathy was rushing toward her, giving her

a thumbs-up sign. "How are you feeling? You look wonderful!" Kathy exclaimed. She knelt down to check Amber's skates, making sure they were just tight enough.

The announcer's voice boomed over the loud-speaker. "Ladies and gentlemen, today is the first day of competition in the junior ladies' division. One group will skate their short program today. The second group will complete this event tomorrow. Today's skaters in the short program will be . . ."

Amber felt a shot of nervous energy as she heard her name. She tried not to look at the packed stands or at the long table where the judges sat. She knew from the announcement that she would be skating first that morning.

"Okay," Kathy said. "It's time for your warm-up. Go on out there and skate your best." Kathy put her arms around her and gave her a big hug.

Amber glided out to the warm-up area and began skating in slow circles, going over her routine in her mind. She practiced a few jumps and spins.

And then it was time.

As she skated to the center of the rink, she forgot that thousands of people were watching her. She forgot that there were TV cameras pointed at her. She forgot that she hated her baby-blue outfit and that it made her look like a little girl. She focused on the music and the routine. And she skated.

Her legs and arms seemed to have a mind of their

own, because when she looked back later, she couldn't remember actually thinking about her moves. She just did them. The step sequence went perfectly. She did her jump combination, the double axel and a triple salchow. She hardly even knew what she was doing. It all just happened so naturally, as if her body knew instinctively what to do.

Then it was time for the double flip. Amber held her breath. She did it! She glided into her final moves, a camel spin, a sit spin, and then into a back sit spin. It seemed as if her program was over before it had begun. How had she looked? she wondered. It had felt good. Really good. But how had it looked?

Her spin slowed to a stop. She heard the applause begin. The noise was incredible. On the sidelines she saw Kathy, Dan, her mother, Haley, and Nikki cheering wildly.

As she took her bows she felt happiness wash over her. She was so proud, she felt as though she might burst. Tears overflowed and ran down her cheeks.

She skated over to the barrier. Everyone started hugging her at once—Kathy and Dan, her mother, and Nikki and Haley.

"Gorgeous!" Kathy exclaimed. "The best I've ever seen you skate!"

"It *was*, honey, I was so impressed," her mother cried.

"Really, Amber, that was terrific!" Haley exclaimed.

"You skate well under pressure, Amber. That's

something that will really help you. Congratulations," Dan told her.

They all waited silently while her score was called out. When the numbers flashed on the signboard, there was another round of cheering and applause. Her marks were high. Amber let out a whoop of excitement.

She searched the bleachers for Tori. She wondered why she wasn't here with the others. Hadn't she been watching?

The next competitor took the ice. Amber turned to watch and spotted Tori peering out from the passageway that led to the warm-up area. Amber hurried over to her.

"So, what did you think?" she asked.

"You looked good. Nice job," Tori said.

"Thanks! It felt great!" Amber cried. "The program went really well—no flubs at all. But I am so glad it's over. What did you think of my triple salchow–double toe loop? I know you've had trouble with yours." She paused. Tori didn't seem to be listening.

"Is something wrong, Tori?" Amber asked.

"No. Nothing's wrong," Tori answered sharply. "But I'm not your coach. Why don't you go talk to Kathy? She's got plenty of time for you."

Amber stared at Tori. She seemed so mad. But why? What had she done? Amber wondered. The day before, Tori had stuck up for her in front of Carla Benson. She had thought Tori was her friend. But now it seemed as if Tori almost hated her. Amber felt close to tears.

She searched for her mother and spotted Mrs. Armstrong standing with Mrs. Carsen in the long passageway. Her mother was talking away, and Mrs. Carsen hardly seemed to be listening. How embarrassing, Amber thought. Why was her mother bothering Mrs. Carsen, anyway?

Tori's mom was wearing flowing gray crepe pants with a matching sash, a cream-colored blouse, and a crepe jacket that matched the pants. She looked stunning and glamorous—as always. Her mother, meanwhile, had on a cheap bright blue pantsuit. Her mother never spent any money on her clothes. Amber knew it was because all her money went to Amber's skating. Suddenly she wished her mother's clothes were a lot nicer.

Mrs. Armstrong turned and motioned Amber over. Amber hurried up to the two women. Her mother put an arm around her shoulders.

"She skated so beautifully. You must be very proud," Mrs. Carsen said.

"I really am." Mrs. Armstrong gave Amber a squeeze. "But Tori is a great skater, too. And she looks lovely today. Is that dress also one of your designs?"

"Yes, it is." Mrs. Carsen turned to watch the next skater take the ice.

"It must be wonderful to be able to sew like that," Mrs. Armstrong went on. "Do you work from a regular pattern? Or do you make up your own designs?"

"I modify a basic pattern," Mrs. Carsen answered crisply.

Why couldn't her mother just be quiet? Amber wondered. Couldn't she see that Mrs. Carsen wasn't the least bit interested in her?

"Do you think your patterns would work for Amber? I don't know—she's so petite next to Tori. Tori already has an adorable figure," Amber's mom said. "I like Amber in sweeter styles, like what she's wearing. Isn't that bow perfect?"

Amber stared at her mother in horror. Mrs. Carsen smiled stiffly and nodded.

This is so embarrassing! Amber thought, squirming. Here I am, wearing the stupidest dress in the world, and my mother is praising it to Mrs. Carsen. Why can't she just leave her alone?

But Mrs. Armstrong kept on asking Mrs. Carsen about Tori's dresses. Finally Mrs. Carsen pulled out her sketchbook. The two women paged through it. Amber could see that it was filled with sketches of skating costumes.

Nikki and Haley noticed what they were doing and hurried over to see the notebook, too.

"I love this one. That would be great on Tori," Nikki cried.

"Look at this one with the long train in back. I've never seen a skating outfit like it," Haley declared.

Tori's so lucky to have a talented mom, Amber thought.

Tori spotted Nikki, came over, and whispered something to her. Nikki nodded. "We're going to get a soda," Tori announced.

"Can I come, too?" Amber asked.

"I think you'd better stay with me, Amber," Mrs. Armstrong said.

Tori and the others left.

"Why do I have to stay here? The others don't have to stay with their mothers all day," Amber complained.

"You're not the others," her mother replied. "Anyway, they've already left and you'll never catch them in this crowd."

Amber gazed at her mother in disbelief. She had just skated a better program than most of the older girls. She *was* like them. They weren't the problem. It was her mother. *She* was the problem. And Amber had to do something about it.

7

Haley—

Our friend the judge is sitting two tables to the left. Maybe we should start a food fight and really impress him!

I don't care if we did get in trouble the other night—it was still fun.

See you after practice.

Alex

As she finished her lunch Haley read Alex's note over again. He had written it on a napkin. He must have left it on her tray while she was at the counter getting a second glass of juice. He and Nikki had to go to practice, so when she came back they were already gone.

It was such a friendly note, funny and cute—just like Alex. Haley felt a special thrill. He had taken time to write her. He was thinking about her. That was a very good sign. Because it seemed to Haley that Alex was on her mind an awful lot lately. She *really* liked him.

Haley folded the napkin carefully and tucked it into the pocket of her jeans. She took a last sip of her juice, cleared her tray, and headed out to the rink to watch Nikki and Alex practice.

Things were not going well. Haley could see that as soon as she sat down. Nikki had that look she always wore when she was unhappy about her skating. There was still a smile plastered across her face because skaters were taught to smile. It was part of the performance. But while her lips were smiling, the rest of her face wasn't.

Usually Nikki and Alex skated naturally together. But as they ran through their short program, they seemed stiff. They were even having trouble staying in sync. Near the end of their routine, Alex's hand slipped as they were going into an overhead lift. Nikki almost fell. Alex caught her in time, but Nikki's smile turned into a scowl.

"Okay. Let's wrap it up for today," Kathy called to them. "Don't worry. You've heard the expression 'A bad practice means a good performance.' The most important thing is to get a good night's sleep tonight. You should be fresh for your short program tomorrow. Once you're out there performing for real, it will all come together."

"I'm going to skate a few laps to cool down," Nikki said.

Alex left the ice and plopped down beside Haley on the bench. "Well, that was a disaster," he grumbled.

"You heard Kathy," Haley said. "A bad practice means a good performance. It's true, too. Remember when Patrick and I won the Regionals? We had the worst practice of our lives the day before."

"Really?"

"Really. He dropped me about five times."

Alex laughed. "I don't remember that."

"Oh, it was pathetic," Haley said, glad to see him laughing. "We were doing a star-lift and I lost my balance and knocked him over. We both ended up flat out on the ice." Haley laughed, too. It was funny now, but it hadn't been funny then. "I think Kathy was about ready to give up on us. But the very next day we won the Regionals."

Nikki had finished her cool-down. She glided off the ice. When she saw Alex and Haley laughing, she glared at them angrily. She stomped past them without saying anything.

"I think she's mad at me," Alex said.

"Why, whatever gave you that idea?" Haley joked. They could both see that Nikki was furious.

"She acts like I'm doing this on purpose. I'm not trying to mess up," Alex said sincerely.

"It's just nerves," Haley replied, trying to reassure him. "You know Nikki. She hates to be less than perfect."

It's too bad Nikki can't lighten up a bit, though, Haley thought. She didn't say it out loud because she didn't want to worry Alex. But if Nikki didn't calm down, she might be too uptight to skate well the next day, when it really mattered.

"What are we doing tonight?" Alex asked as they walked back to the hotel.

"There's some kind of dinner and reception again," Haley told him.

"Another one of those boring things?"

"Yeah. And this one should be *really* exciting," Haley said sarcastically. "I hear the national figure-skating champion from something like 1937 is going to give a speech."

"Oh, man," Alex groaned. "How boring." He kicked at a stone in the road. "Hey, I just remembered something. This kid told me about a party tonight in the hotel. They have one every year. Want to go there instead?"

"Sounds cool," Haley said, trying to hide her excitement.

Was this like a date, she wondered, or just a friendly invitation? She hoped it was a date!

"Let's meet in the lobby after everyone else has gone over to the reception, say around seven," Alex said.

"Okay. See you later."

Haley flew back to her room. Nikki was in the shower. Haley reached for her hairbrush and noticed a valentine note on the bureau. "Nikki, keep your heart set on your goal," it said.

Cool, Haley thought. Nikki's got a secret admirer! She couldn't wait for Nikki to get out of the shower so she could ask her about it.

Haley flopped down on the bed and stared dreamily at the ceiling. Maybe they would both end up with valentines! What an incredible week this could be!

Nikki popped out of the bathroom in a robe, her hair wrapped in a towel.

"Hey! You didn't tell me you had a valentine. What's going on?" Haley teased.

"What are you talking about?" Nikki asked. She tripped over a pile of Haley's clothes and frowned.

"That valentine note, 'Keep your heart set on your goal.' Who's it from?"

"Oh, I don't know. Probably someone trying to make me feel better about how badly we're skating." Nikki combed through her tangled hair.

"Remember what Kathy said, 'A bad practice—' "

"If I hear that once more, I'm going to scream!" Nikki exploded before Haley could finish. She turned and tripped over Haley's backpack, which was lying on the floor. "There's plenty of drawer space, you know. Why don't you put some of your stuff away before someone has an accident?"

"Hey, I'm sorry. You know what a slob I am. I'll put it away later," Haley promised.

"Yeah, I can see how busy you are," Nikki snapped.

"What's that supposed to mean?" Haley asked.

"Nothing." Nikki turned her back and began blow-drying her hair.

She's just nervous about tomorrow, Haley thought. She needs something to take her mind off it. Like a party!

"Listen," she said when Nikki turned off her hair dryer, "there's a big party tonight in the hotel. Want to come?"

"Tonight? We can't. We have that reception."

"No one will care if we skip it," Haley assured her. "It sounds so boring. I'm sick of those things, and so is Alex. We're allowed to have some fun, too."

"We might get into trouble if we skip the reception. Kathy and Dan might notice we're not there," Nikki warned. She slipped into a short flowered dress.

"Maybe not," Haley said.

"Look, I know you're not competing, but I am. And so is Alex. We need to get to bed early. It would be really stupid to ruin our skating for a party."

"One party is not going to ruin your skating," Haley insisted.

"That's right. Because I'm not going. And I don't think Alex should go, either," Nikki retorted.

"Well, I guess that's up to Alex, isn't it?"

"Yeah. And I wish you'd leave him alone. Let him

focus on his skating. No wonder he's doing badly. You keep distracting him."

"What? Distracting him? Are you crazy?" Haley blurted out. "This party was his idea! I'm just trying to help him relax so he can do well tomorrow."

"Well, do me a favor. Quit trying to help!" Nikki yelled. "We'd be better off if you just left him alone."

Haley was so angry she grabbed her hairbrush and flung it onto the floor next to her backpack.

"I'm ready," Nikki snapped. "Are you coming or not?"

The last thing Haley felt like doing was going anywhere with Nikki.

"I've got a headache now," she fibbed. "I'll just stay here."

Nikki checked the mirror one more time and picked up her key. She kicked one of Haley's tennis shoes out of her way and left without saying another word.

Who does Nikki think she is, anyway? Haley fumed. She stormed into the bathroom and turned on the shower. Nikki wasn't going to stop her. She was definitely going on what might be her first-ever date with Alex!

8

Haley checked the mirror one more time. She had showered, blow-dried her red hair, and put on the new outfit she had just bought at Canady's: loose white pants and a black stretchy top. It was time to meet Alex in the lobby. She was excited and also kind of nervous. She wasn't sure how she should act. Did Alex just want her for a friend? Or was he beginning to feel that there was something more between them? Maybe that night she would find out.

She only hoped Nikki didn't find out that they were going to the party. She felt bad about lying to her. But really, Nikki was being such a pain. Why shouldn't they go out and have a good time?

Haley brushed her hair again and then searched for her key. She sifted through the pile of junk on the bureau. She really should clean up sometime, she thought, but not now. She found her key in the pocket of the pants she had worn earlier that day. A few minutes later she was waiting for Alex in the lobby.

He wasn't there yet. Maybe he'd changed his mind, she thought. Maybe Nikki had gotten to him first. Maybe she'd told him not to go to the party. Haley felt sick. He wasn't going to show up! Then she saw him get off the elevator and glance around for her.

"Alex," she cried. She was so glad to see him.

"Hi," he said. "Ready to go?"

"Definitely." She hesitated. Should she warn him that Nikki wasn't too happy about their going to the party? She decided she had to say something.

"Listen," she began, "I just want to warn you. Nikki didn't think this party was such a great idea. You might not want to tell her about it."

"Really? What's the big deal?" Alex asked. "It's just a party."

Haley was so happy to hear he felt the same way she did. She almost hugged him.

"That's exactly what I think," Haley said. "But you know how Nikki's been lately. Kind of uptight and all."

"Kind of? I've never seen her this nervous! I don't know what it is. We've both worked so hard to get here. I guess she feels a lot more pressure than I do."

"Maybe that's it," Haley said. "Anyway, I asked her

if she wanted to come with us tonight. I thought it might cheer her up. But she got all bent out of shape. She started saying we were going to get in trouble and we might ruin your skating tomorrow. Finally I told her I had a headache and was going to stay in the room. I hate lying to her, but . . ."

Alex nodded. "Hey, let's not worry about Nikki or anyone else right now. This party sounds cool. Lots of people are going to be there."

Haley felt a thrill of excitement ripple through her. She was going to a cool party with Alex! Who cared what Nikki thought?

They took the elevator up to the twelfth floor.

"Room twelve-fifty-one," Alex said. "That's this way."

They hadn't gone far when they began to hear noise, music, and voices floating through the hall.

"Hear that? It must be the party," Alex said.

They turned a corner, and the noise grew louder. People spilled out into the hall from an open door. One couple sat against the wall outside the door, having a serious conversation. They didn't seem to notice the noisy crowd around them. Another boy stood by himself. "It's crazy in there," he told them.

Haley and Alex stopped outside the door and peered into the room.

"It's wall-to-wall people," Haley agreed.

"Do you see anyone we know?" Alex asked.

"A couple of kids I met today," Haley answered. "And there's Brett Mason. He's a member of Blade Runners. I wonder if Carla Benson's here."

"There's Dave. He's the guy who invited me." Alex waved to a lanky boy with dark curly hair.

Dave hurried over. "Hey! Come on in. There're soft drinks on the table across the room. If you can get over there, help yourself." Dave laughed. "I'm glad you made it."

Then he was gone, following someone else through the crowd. The room was really a suite, with a bedroom off the living room. The bedroom was also filled with people.

Haley spotted a long table loaded with soft drinks, pretzels, and chips. The TV was tuned to a local cable station showing highlights of the day's skating events. A group of people was glued to the set, laughing and commenting. Haley joined them while Alex went to get their drinks. The TV flickered. There was a close-up of a young skater.

"Hey, that's Amber!" Haley cried.

"She's great. Who is she?" said a girl standing near Haley.

"Amber Armstrong. She's a member of Silver Blades," Haley said proudly.

"Silver Blades? I've heard of them. A good club," the girl said. She was tall and slender, and her black hair was cut very short. "I'm Francie Morrell. I go to the International Ice Academy in Denver."

"The Ice Academy!" Haley cried. "Then you must know Jill! Jill Wong?"

"Sure, I know Jill. Too bad she hurt her foot and couldn't compete to enter the Nationals. She would definitely have qualified," Francie said. "Do you know her well?"

"Sure! We skated together in Silver Blades. She's one of my best friends. My name's Haley, by the way. Haley Arthur."

"So you're with Silver Blades, too?"

Haley nodded. "I skate pairs. But I'm not skating in the competition. I'm here for support."

"Wow. It's great of you to come," Francie said. "It's a long trip for you."

Haley was about to explain more when Alex returned with their Cokes. Haley introduced him to Francie.

The three of them chatted for a while. Francie introduced them to a couple of new people. Alex soon had them laughing. Haley had forgotten all about being nervous. She was having a great time.

Haley was joking with a girl she knew from Blade Runners when she glanced at her watch. Oh, no! she thought. Nikki and the others would be back from the reception any minute. She had better get back to the room before Nikki did.

She searched for Alex. He was in a corner talking to Francie Morrell. He laughed at something Francie said, and Haley felt a pang of jealousy. She hadn't really spent much time with Alex, and now it was time to leave.

She pushed her way through the crowd to where he and Francie were standing.

"Alex, it's almost ten. They'll be back from the reception any minute," Haley said. "We've got to go. I don't want Nikki to find out we came here."

Alex turned to Francie. "We were supposed to go to that reception tonight," he explained.

"Me too," Francie said. "In fact, if Ludmila finds out I skipped it, I'll be in big trouble. But a party sounded like much more fun. Those receptions are getting boring."

"Really boring," Alex agreed. "I'm glad we didn't go." He nudged Francie's arm. "And I'm glad we met you. Will you be around tomorrow?"

"Yes. Do you want to—"

"Well, we've got to go," Haley interrupted. "Give Jill a hug for me," she told Francie.

"Oh, sure. Hope I see you tomorrow," Francie said. She smiled at Alex.

"Definitely," Alex responded. Haley could tell that he liked Francie . . . maybe a little too much. She pulled Alex away.

The party had spilled out into the hall, and it showed no signs of breaking up.

"That was fun. I'm really glad we went," Haley said.

"Hey, you guys. What are you doing here?" Tori's voice rang out. Haley remembered that Tori's room was on this floor. "Nikki told me you were sick," Tori said. She frowned as she hurried toward them.

"I, uh . . ." Haley stopped and gulped. "Oh, no!" she cried.

Dr. Lawrence appeared, followed by two security guards. In a moment he was beside them.

"Not you again!" Dr. Lawrence recognized Tori, Alex, and Haley. "I should have known you'd be involved in this. You should have been at the reception." He was fuming.

"*I* was at the recep—," Tori tried to say, but he cut her off.

"This noise is disrupting the entire hotel. We assured the hotel management that our skaters were well behaved and responsible. You've made it clear that you're only here for a good time. You don't take your skating very seriously," Dr. Lawrence scolded. "But there are plenty of other skaters who do."

"But I—but—," Tori stuttered. But the skating judge stomped off to break up the party.

"Come on! Let's get out of here," Alex cried. The three of them hurried down the hall.

"I can't believe this!" Tori's eyes flashed. "You guys skipped the reception to go to some stupid party. And now we're all in trouble. Haley, just because you're not skating doesn't mean you can cause trouble!" Tori's face was red with anger. "You should have stayed home."

"Calm down, Tori. It's not that big a deal. It was just

a party. It's not like we did anything really bad," Alex said.

"But the judge already hates us. He'll never forgive us now." Tori's voice trembled as she spoke.

"He'll be judging you on your skating. And that's all," Alex insisted. "Judges can't let their personal feelings get in the way."

"I'm really sorry, Tori. We didn't mean to get you involved," Haley apologized.

Tori rushed to her room door. "Well, thanks for nothing!" She went inside and slammed the door behind her.

Haley felt terrible. She followed Alex to the elevator in silence. They entered and rode down to Haley's floor.

"Nikki's mad at me, and now Tori hates me, too. Maybe I *should* have stayed home," Haley burst out.

Alex squeezed her hand. "No way! I'm glad you came."

"Really?"

He squeezed her hand again and turned to face her. "Really."

At least Alex was still her friend. Maybe more than a friend? she wondered. I wish he would kiss me, she suddenly thought. She felt her cheeks burn. The elevator jerked to a stop and the doors slid open. They were at her floor.

"Well, I'll see you tomorrow," Haley said awkwardly. Her heart was pounding. Why had the elevator stopped just at that moment? Maybe Alex had been about to kiss her. If only she knew what his feelings were.

"I had a great time," Alex said. He flipped her a wave as the elevator door slid shut again.

Haley walked down the hall in a daze. Alex was so cute and so much fun. She didn't care what Tori said. The party had been worth it. *I just hope Nikki doesn't find out,* she thought as she unlocked her door. But as she stepped inside she saw that Nikki was already there.

"Where were you?" Nikki asked in concern. Then she noticed how Haley was dressed. Her eyes narrowed.

"I thought you had a headache," she said.

Haley gulped. "Um . . . would you believe I had a miraculous recovery?"

9

Dear valentine,
*   Could you meet me tonight at nine o'clock in the
hotel lobby?*

Signed,
???????

Tori put down her pen and stared at the note she
had just written. She sat at the little table in her hotel
room drinking a cup of tea. Her mother was in the
shower. That day she would skate her short program.
She was trying not to think too much about it. She
had been skating her best at practice. Now, if only the
judges thought so. . . .

Tori picked up the pen again and began doodling
little hearts with "Pierce + Tori" inside. Was it a bad

idea to send him a valentine note? What if he didn't want to meet her in the hotel lobby? Was the note too pushy? She frowned. Pierce had said he wanted to see her again. What should she do?

If he came to see her skate that day, that would be a definite sign that he liked her. Tori decided to wait until later to send the note. She hid it in the drawer of her bedside table. She called to her mother to hurry. It was time to get to the rink!

As they rushed to the arena, her mother issued a whole list of instructions. "Remember to look at the audience and smile. Don't forget to keep your arms in tight on your toe loop. Make sure that right boot is laced correctly. Don't lean too far back on the layback. Remember to keep your chin up when you do your sit spin. Be sure you don't drop your hip when you land your axel. . . ."

On and on Mrs. Carsen went, until Tori felt like screaming. But instead of screaming she simply tuned her out. She imagined her mother was talking in fast-forward, her voice getting higher and higher and faster and faster. Tori almost started to laugh.

The minute they set foot inside the arena, Dan rushed over to them. "Tori, you look beautiful. Absolutely gorgeous." He beamed. "I have a good feeling about today. You're going to do terrific, I know it. Remember, we're all behind you one hundred percent."

Tori rolled her eyes. Dan said that to everyone, it

seemed. Her mother and Dan chatted nervously as Tori laced up her boots. She felt a burst of apprehension. This is it. This is really it. I'm about to skate in the Nationals. She couldn't believe it was actually happening.

She finished her warm-up feeling relaxed. Then it was time to wait for her turn to compete. Waiting was the worst part. Tori gazed around the narrow passageway that led out to the rink. Carla Benson was on the ice performing her short program. Tori tried not to listen to the reactions of the crowd.

She never watched any skater who performed right before she did—it made her too nervous. If they did well, she was afraid she would do badly. If they did badly, she was afraid she would, too. And it was ten times worse when the skater was someone she really wanted to beat—such as Carla.

There was loud applause as Carla finished her program. Tori covered her ears so she wouldn't hear Carla's marks announced. She squeezed her eyes shut and ran through her own program in her mind.

Dan tapped her on the shoulder. "Get ready," he told her.

Tori heard her name announced. "Next up, Tori Carsen, skating with the Silver Blades Skating Club of Seneca Hills, Pennsylvania."

"This is it, Tori!" Her mother gave her a quick hug.

Dan squeezed her hand. "Just remember, you're going to skate your best."

Tori hurried out to the rink.

"Good luck, Tori. You can do it!" Tori gazed at the stands to her left. She noticed Nikki, Haley, Alex, and Amber sitting there. Tori glanced away from Haley. She was still angry with her—and worried about her marks from Dr. Lawrence.

She glided onto the ice. Her music started, and before she knew it she was skating. Her program was set to music from *The Phantom of the Opera*. It was music that made her feel strong and confident. She went into her first jump, landed it beautifully, and went into a spin.

Next came an impressive footwork sequence. Then came the toughest part of her program: a demanding jump combination of a triple loop followed by a double toe loop.

The triple loop was her weakest jump. She had just started landing it consistently. Her timing had to be perfect. She launched into the jump. As she came out of the triple, she wobbled and almost touched down. Tori forced herself to smile.

Without missing a beat, she reached back and put her toe in strongly and went up into the double toe loop. She performed it flawlessly. She finished her program, ending with a whirlwind layback spin. In the stands her friends clapped and cheered wildly. She skated to the barrier and suddenly her friends were there. They hugged her and told her it was the best she had ever done. She was sure to get a high score.

Haley's eyes met hers. Then her marks were announced.

"Yes!" Tori screamed. Her marks were high. Tori hoped they were better than Carla's. At least Tori and Amber had almost tied, though Amber's marks were slightly higher. Tori vowed to do better in her long program. Still, she felt a wave of relief. Pierce was right. His dad had marked her fairly after all.

Was Pierce there? she wondered. Had he seen her skate? She scanned the arena, trying to spot him. He could be anywhere. There were so many people, she wasn't sure she'd be able to find him in the crowd. But then she saw him. He was staring directly at her. She waved, and he waved back, giving her a thumbs-up sign.

"Excuse me, miss. Are you Tori Carsen?" an usher asked.

"Yes?"

He handed her a long white box. "This is for you."

Tori tore the lid off the box. Inside was one beautiful red rose.

"Wow! That's so romantic," Amber said.

"There's a note," Haley told her.

Tori opened the note and read, "Congratulations! You were beautiful!"

"Who's it from?" Amber asked.

Tori turned the little card over. "It's unsigned. But it must be from Pierce," she cried. "He was waving to me just before the usher delivered this." She searched the stands again, but Pierce was gone.

"Just in time for Valentine's Day!" Haley exclaimed. "You're so lucky."

She *was* lucky. She'd just done great in her short program. Pierce was good-looking, and so romantic, too. What more could she ask for?

Tori rested in her hotel room after lunch. Her mother had insisted she nap before the afternoon practice. But Tori was too excited to sleep. Something small and white on the bureau caught her eye. Tori leaped up and grabbed it. Another note!

"Keep your heart set on your goal," the note said.

Pierce must have sent it before she skated! She had missed it because she and her mother had left so early. Now she knew he cared about her. She should definitely send him the valentine she had written that morning.

She found an envelope, rescued the note from its hiding place, and tucked it inside. She wrote Pierce's name and room number on the envelope. When she went to seal it, she noticed that the glue was kind of old. It didn't seem to stick properly. Oh, well, she thought. It's just going within the hotel, so it will be all right.

Tori placed the note on her bureau next to another note that her mother had asked her to drop off at the front desk. I've got to remember to take these next time I go downstairs, she told herself.

She smiled happily. What a great day, she thought. First her triumph on the ice, and then all this attention from Pierce. Things couldn't get much better.

10

Dear Jana,

Remember how we used to pretend that we were skating in the Nationals? Well, guess where I am. I made it! And I'm doing well! My short program went great, and I skate my long program in two days.

I've been working really hard. I joined Silver Blades, and there are some cool kids in the club. My best friend is Tori Carsen. She's really pretty and fun. Not as much fun as you, though. I miss you.

Love,
Amber

P.S. I just got a card from an anonymous valentine!

Amber remembered how she and Jana used to dress up in their best skating outfits and play "Nationals." One of them would be the announcer while the other one would "skate," which meant sliding around in their stocking feet on the shiny linoleum floor in Jana's basement. And now here she was.

Amber really wished that Jana were here, too. She missed her. She and Jana had been close friends since the first day of nursery school. There was no one else who knew her as well, even though Amber had become serious about skating and Jana hadn't.

When she thought about it, she also missed her old life back in New Mexico, when they had lived like a normal family, in a regular house. Her dad was still living there. He hadn't been able to leave his job. It was hard for Amber and her mom to live apart from him.

But right now her skating was more important than anything else. It was worth sacrificing for. And anyway, she was starting to make friends in Silver Blades. Tori was her friend, and she was so cool. Cooler than Jana would ever be.

"Sweetie? Are you getting ready?" Amber's mother called from the bathroom. "It's almost time to go back to the rink for your afternoon practice session."

"Mom, Tori's going over, too. I told her I'd go with her. So you don't need to come, okay?" This wasn't quite true. Tori was going over to the rink, but Amber hadn't talked to her about their going together. Tori won't mind, though, Amber told herself. She likes me.

"But I want to go with you," her mother said. "I want to watch you practice your long program."

"You can. But I'd rather go over there with Tori. If it's okay with you." Amber waited for an answer.

Her mother hesitated. "Well, I guess it's okay. But let's make sure Tori knows she's in charge of you." She reached for the telephone, but Amber stopped her.

"Mom, please! You can't tell Tori she's in charge of me!" Amber exclaimed. "How old do you think I am? I'm not five. I can take care of myself."

"Well, if you promise you'll stay with the other girls," her mother finally said.

"I promise," Amber assured her.

"All right, then. You go ahead. I'll be along later."

"Thanks, Mom." Amber gave her a quick kiss, grabbed her skating bag, and hurried to Tori's room.

She knocked on the door. Tori called, "Coming!"

Amber waited, and in a minute Tori opened the door. She was in her bathrobe.

"Oh," Tori said. "I thought you were Nikki. I wanted to wish her luck before her short program later." Amber could hear the disappointment in Tori's voice.

"Are you going over to practice soon? Can I go with you?" Amber asked.

"Yeah, I guess so." Tori stepped back and opened the door wider so Amber could come in. "I'm still getting changed, so you'll have to wait a few minutes."

"That's okay," Amber said as Tori disappeared into the bathroom.

Amber looked around the room. It was almost like the one she was sharing with her mother, but a bit bigger. Tori had a view of the skating arena across the road. It was better than Amber's view of the office building next door.

Amber wandered aimlessly around the room. Her eyes fell on the two notes on Tori's bureau. She looked more closely at them and saw that one had Pierce's name on it. A valentine? she wondered. She knew she shouldn't snoop, but she couldn't resist. The envelope wasn't sealed or anything.

She slipped the note out of the envelope and read it. A valentine meeting—how romantic!

And there was another valentine. It was addressed to Roger in Mrs. Carsen's handwriting. She opened it and read, "Let me be your number one and you won't regret it."

"I'll be right out!" Tori called.

Uh-oh! A wave of panic swept over Amber. She couldn't let Tori catch her snooping. Quickly she stuffed the notes back into the envelopes and rushed over to the window, pretending she had been there all along.

Tori came out of the bathroom dressed for skating.

Even though it was just a practice session, Tori wore a beautiful emerald green skating dress. "Ready?" she called, pulling on her Silver Blades warm-up jacket. "We'd better hurry. There's not much practice time before the pairs short program." She grabbed the two notes and her key, and Amber followed her out into the hall.

"I have to stop at the front desk and mail these," Tori said. Amber felt bad that she had snooped, but at least Tori hadn't caught her.

Dan was already on the ice when they got to the rink.

"Right on time, girls," he said when he saw them. "Kathy is working with Nikki and Alex on their short program. They'll need extra attention before they compete later. But let's get you warmed up. Only two more practice sessions before your long programs."

They glided out onto the ice and began warming up. Amber wanted to talk to Tori as they stroked around the rink, but Tori was silent. Amber thought she knew why. All the singles skaters had finished competing in the short program, and their official rankings had been announced.

Amber had placed fourth. Carla had placed fifth. And Tori had placed behind both of them. She was in sixth place—and furious about it.

Amber and Tori finished their warm-ups and glided over to Dan.

"Okay, Amber, you can begin your routine," he said.

"Tori, I want you to work on the timing when you come out of the flying camel and down into your back sit spin. Let's try to make that transition as smooth as possible."

Amber started to run through her long program. She felt good that day, relaxed and strong. Every jump seemed to flow smoothly into the next one. She finished her program without one mistake and began to circle the rink.

Amber glanced over at Tori and Dan. Things weren't going so well for Tori. She opened her arms out too soon on her double axel and almost lost her balance. She had trouble regaining her composure.

"Oh, no!" Tori exploded. "I've only got two more days. The way I'm skating today, I'm going to blow my long program. What should I do?"

"Tori, one bad practice is not the end of the world," Dan assured her. "Everyone has a bad day now and then. Just relax. Why don't you do some skating just for fun? Work on some easy things and relax."

"What good will that do? I've got to get this program down," Tori snapped.

"You've got it down," Dan assured Tori. "It's just nerves. The best solution is to relax and enjoy yourself."

Amber decided to run through her program once again. As she began skating she noticed a woman watching her closely from the stands.

Dan glided up to Amber and stood watching while

she completed her program. When she was done, he applauded. "What can I say? You don't need me today. If you skate like that in the real event, you'll place high."

The ice was suddenly crowded. Their time was up. Dan called Tori over. "Okay, we've got to let someone else have a chance. Good job." He threw an arm around Tori's shoulder, but she shrugged it off.

"Good job? Are you crazy?" she muttered.

"Now, Tori, you just need to relax."

"Why do you keep saying that?" Tori cried. "Why can't you act like a real coach and explain what I'm doing wrong?"

She skated over to where Nikki and Alex were speaking with Kathy. Amber noticed that Nikki seemed more nervous than ever. She and Alex were the only ones in their group who hadn't skated their short program yet. Amber saw Tori murmur a word of encouragement to Nikki. Then Tori turned away, frowning.

Amber and Dan stared after her. "Tori doesn't look too happy," Amber remarked.

Dan smiled. "You watch," he said. "She'll be terrific when it's the real thing."

As Amber was taking off her skates, the woman who had been watching her from the stands approached.

"Hi, Amber," she said with a smile.

"Hi," Amber said, wondering who the woman was and how she knew her name.

"My name is Roberta Jamison. I'm a reporter for *Sports Illustrated For Kids*. Have you seen our magazine?"

"Sure. Everyone has," Amber said.

"Well, that's good news. I was watching your practice. You skated beautifully. I could see that your coach was very pleased."

Amber shrugged. "I guess so."

The woman sat down next to her. "Listen, Amber. My magazine has asked me to do a feature on young athletes, and I'd very much like to include you. What do you think?"

"You mean, I'd be in *Sports Illustrated For Kids*?" Amber asked.

"That's right," Roberta replied.

"Wow! That'd be cool," Amber cried.

"Great. I'll need to interview you. And we'll have to set up a time for a photo shoot," Roberta explained. "Do you have a few minutes now? Maybe we could get started on the interview. Don't worry—I'll give a copy to your mom before we make this final. Okay?"

"Sure. I'm kind of thirsty, though," Amber admitted.

"I guess you would be after that workout. Let's get you a drink and then we'll talk. Okay?"

Amber followed the reporter to the snack bar in the lounge. "What would you like, Amber?"

Amber took her wallet out of her skating bag.

"No. My treat," Roberta said. "Just tell me what you want."

"I'll have lemonade," Amber said.

"Anything to eat? You must burn a lot of calories out there."

"No, thanks," Amber answered.

"One lemonade and a diet Coke," Roberta told the boy behind the counter. When the drinks came, she paid and handed Amber her lemonade. "Let's sit over here and talk," she said, leading Amber to two cozy chairs.

Roberta unzipped her briefcase and took out a pad of paper, a pencil, and a tiny tape recorder. "You don't mind if I tape our conversation, do you, Amber? It makes it easier when I'm writing. And I'll let your mom listen to this."

Amber had been interviewed a couple of times before, so she was comfortable being recorded.

"Well, let's start at the beginning," Roberta began. "Why don't you tell me all about how you first began skating?"

Amber loved to talk. She had just gotten to the part where she'd met her first coach back in New Mexico when suddenly Tori rushed over to her.

"Amber! There you are. I've been looking for you!"

"You have?" Amber was surprised. Tori's mood sure had changed.

"Yeah. I thought we could grab a snack together."

"Well, actually," Roberta cut in, "we're doing an interview right now. Do you think you can spare your friend for a few minutes?"

"An interview?" Tori pulled another chair up and sat down. "Maybe I can help. Amber and I are in the same club. And we're friends, too." She beamed at Amber.

"That's true," Amber said.

Tori leaned closer and nudged Amber's shoulder. "Amber's a terrific skater. Together, we're an unbeatable team."

Roberta scribbled some notes.

Wow, Amber thought. Tori and me, an unbeatable team! Amber wanted more than anything to believe that Tori was truly her friend. But she couldn't help wondering if Tori really meant what she said about being a great team or if she just wanted to be part of the interview.

As she listened to Tori trying to impress Roberta, Amber had a feeling she knew the answer.

11

Jill! Valentine update—

I met the most incredible guy, Pierce Lawrence. He's great-looking, and he's really sweet. He sent me a rose to congratulate me on my short program. I'm going to meet him for almost a real date later tonight!

I'll keep you posted.

Love,
Tori

P.S. You should send a cheer-up note to Nikki— and fast! She and Alex didn't do too well in their short program today. I just hope they skate well in their long program.

It was a few minutes before nine o'clock at night. Tori raced to the elevator. She was going to meet Pierce downstairs in the hotel lobby. Luckily, her mother was meeting Roger for dinner that night. She had already dressed and left their room, leaving Tori a few minutes to change her clothes. She had decided on a short white skirt and a blue knit top. She'd tied her hair to one side and added a dab of lipstick.

Will he be there? she asked herself as she reached the lobby. Did he get my note?

Tori sat down on one of the plush gray couches. From there she had a view of the front doors to the hotel and the elevator. She'd be sure to see him whichever way he entered.

She picked up a copy of *Time* magazine from the table beside the couch. She leafed through it, but she couldn't concentrate. She put down the magazine, jumped up, and began pacing around the lobby.

She stood in front of the newsstand and browsed. She wandered to the information desk and leafed through the activity pamphlets. She checked her watch. It was five minutes past nine. Well, he was only a few minutes late. He could have gotten held up somewhere or lost track of the time. He would be along, she was sure of it.

She wandered back to the couch and sat down. She had just picked up the magazine again when she felt a hand on her shoulder.

Pierce! she thought, turning around happily.

"Roger!" she shrieked. He was the last person she wanted to see.

"Hi, Tori. Did I startle you? I'm sorry, I thought you'd be expecting me."

"Oh . . . you did? I mean, I was . . . I mean . . ."

"Your mom sent you, didn't she? Is she running late?"

"Mom?" Tori had no idea what he was talking about.

"Yes. I was supposed to meet her here. I assumed she sent you to tell me she was going to be late. You know how she is." He smiled. "Punctuality just isn't her strong point."

"B-But I thought you were having dinner together," Tori stammered. Her mother had left their room before Tori to meet Roger in the hotel restaurant. Tori had been relieved that her mother wouldn't know she was meeting Pierce.

"Well, yes, but she sent me a note asking me to meet her here instead," Roger said.

Tori glanced at her watch. It was ten minutes past nine. How was she going to get rid of Roger? She didn't want him to see that she was meeting Pierce. He'd tell her mom. And her mother wouldn't approve. She scanned the lobby, but Pierce was nowhere in sight.

"Maybe you should check the restaurant," Tori suggested. "I know she was planning to meet you there. She left our room about half an hour ago."

"Really?" Roger seemed confused. "How strange. But I guess I'd better have a look."

Good, thought Tori. That would take care of Roger.

But just as he was about to leave she heard her mother call from across the lobby. "Roger! There you are! I've been waiting for you in the restaurant. What happened?" Her mother marched toward them. "Did you forget?" she demanded.

"Forget? Of course I didn't forget." Roger squeezed her hand. His voice got that sickeningly sweet tone that Tori hated. "As if I could ever forget a date with you."

Tori's mother gazed back at him. The two of them stood there staring at each other with the dumbest expressions Tori had ever seen. She cleared her throat to remind them that she was still there.

They glanced at her in surprise. Roger said, "No harm done."

"But what about our big dinner plans?" Mrs. Carsen frowned.

"Yes, that's why I'm here," Roger said.

"But we agreed we'd meet in the restaurant."

"Oh, stop it!" Tori cried. She had to get them out of there before Pierce showed up. He was already fifteen minutes late. Her mother and Roger stared at her in surprise.

"I mean, you found each other—that's the important thing. You'd better get to the restaurant. They might cancel your reservation," Tori said in a calmer tone of voice.

Roger checked his watch. "She's right. We'd better get going."

"Yes, but Tori, what are you doing down here?" her mother asked. "I thought you were going to watch TV in the room and get a good night's sleep."

"Um, well, I was, but . . ." She had to think of an excuse quickly. Luckily, she spotted Nikki across the lobby at that moment. She waved to her. "Nikki called and said to meet her here," Tori fibbed. She rushed over and grabbed Nikki. "Here she is! See you later."

She dragged Nikki into the coffee shop on the other side of the lobby. Her mother and Roger couldn't see it from the restaurant they would be going to.

"Whew, that was close! Thank goodness you showed up when you did," Tori cried as they slid into a booth.

"I wanted to see if my family was here yet. They're flying in tonight. They really wanted to be here for my long program, day after tomorrow." Nikki frowned.

"Too bad they weren't here for your short program," Tori said.

Nikki shrugged. "I was kind of upset at first that my dad couldn't get away from his job. That's why they weren't here earlier. But now I'm kind of glad they didn't see me skate so badly."

"Maybe you'll do better when they *are* here," Tori suggested.

Nikki brightened. "Yeah, maybe. Anyway, what's going on with you?"

Tori explained about meeting Pierce and how her mother and Roger had shown up instead. Suddenly Nikki squeezed her arm. "Quiet," Nikki whispered. "Don't say another word."

"Why? What is it?"

"Behind you. Don't turn around."

"What?"

"It's Pierce. Sitting at a table right near us."

"Pierce Lawrence?"

"Shhh," Nikki hissed. "He'll hear you." She ducked her head. "He's looking right at us. I think he saw us."

"Why are you hiding?" Tori began to stand up. "He was supposed to meet me in the lobby at nine."

"But . . . he's with another girl," Nikki blurted out.

"He is?" Tori felt her stomach drop.

"Shhh." Nikki glanced back. "The girl's getting up. She's heading to the ladies' room."

"What's Pierce doing?" Tori asked.

"He's getting up, too." Nikki picked up a menu from the table. "Pretend we're thinking about ordering." They buried their heads in the menu.

Pierce strolled over to them. "Tori! Hi."

"Uh, hi, Pierce." Tori was confused. Pierce seemed surprised to see her. She didn't know what to say. Had he stood her up? Had he even gotten her note? Suddenly she wished she hadn't sent it. Should she ask him about it?

"Have you guys eaten? Do you want to come and sit with us? I'm with a friend. Her parents are good friends of my parents. It's sort of a favor to my dad," Pierce explained.

"Um, I've already eaten," Nikki said.

"We were just curious about the menu in case we ever might want to eat here . . . you know, some other time," Tori rambled on. "I really like to look at menus." What a dumb thing to say, Tori thought. He must think I'm crazy.

"Oh. Well, do you want to join us anyway?" Pierce asked.

"No, we can't," Nikki said.

Tori was dying to ask him about the note. But if he had gotten it, he would say something about it, wouldn't he? Wouldn't he explain why he hadn't met her? And if he hadn't gotten it, she didn't want him to know she'd sent it. She decided not to say anything.

"Yeah, we'd better go," she mumbled.

"Listen, Tori. Do you want to do something tomorrow night? A movie or something?" Pierce asked.

Tori couldn't believe it. He was asking her on a date! "Yes. Yes, I'd love to."

"Great. I'll see you at the rink tomorrow. We'll figure out what time and all."

"Okay. Great."

Pierce went back to his table. Nikki and Tori hurried out of the coffee shop. As they crossed the lobby toward the elevator, Tori felt as if she were floating.

"He asked me on a date. A real date. Oh, wow! Isn't he the best-looking thing you've ever seen?"

"He *is* handsome," Nikki said. "But there's something about him . . . Do you really think that girl was just a friend of his family?"

"Of course. Why would he ask me out if he already has a girlfriend?"

Nikki shrugged. "I don't know," she said. "There's just something about him. It's like he's almost too smooth, you know?"

"No, I don't know. You're too suspicious."

"Yeah, maybe," Nikki said.

A date with Pierce! Tori couldn't believe her luck. If only she didn't have to skate her long program the day after their date. She knew her mother—and Dan—would never approve of her going out the night before she competed.

Well, she would make sure she got home early. Pierce would understand. No way was she going to give up a date with him. Not for anything.

12

Dear Dani,

I'm not sure what's going on with Alex and me. One minute I think he likes me, and the next I don't. I'm confused. I wish we could hang out alone for once. One thing I do know is how I feel. This is one serious crush. . . .

Meanwhile, Nikki is being a real pain. I'm trying to be sympathetic because I know she's nervous. But it's not easy!

The next time you see me, I will either be in heaven or have a broken heart!

Love,
Haley

The next morning Haley woke up late. Nikki was already gone. It was their last full day of practice. The following day they would all skate their long programs. Haley knew Nikki wanted to get an early start that morning. On the table by the bed was a note. Haley picked it up and read: "Haley, I've gone to the rink. N."

Not too friendly. Was she still mad that Haley and Alex had gone to the party the other night? Haley frowned. She sat up and glanced around.

Nikki's side of the room was spotless. When did she get to be such a neat freak? Haley wondered. Nikki had always been organized, but not like this. The maid would be in later to tidy up, but Nikki had already made her bed. That's just plain weird, Haley thought.

Then she noticed that there was a pile of her stuff in the corner. Nikki must have stacked it there. If she wants to obsess about her own things, it's her business, Haley thought. But does she have to mess with mine?

Haley felt a pang of guilt. Maybe it's because her parents have finally gotten here. They'll probably want to see her room today. So I guess I should put my junk away, Haley thought.

She climbed out of bed and surveyed the mess. Her stomach growled. I'm starved. Can't work on an empty stomach, she told herself. I'll clean it all after breakfast and surprise Nikki.

Haley washed and dressed and headed downstairs. As she stepped out of the elevator, she ran into Tori.

"Hi. I'm just going to get breakfast," Haley said. "Want to come?"

"I just ate, but guess what!"

"What?" Haley asked.

"I've got a date tonight! With Pierce Lawrence!"

"Really? He called you?"

"I ran into him last night and he invited me."

"That's so cool. He's really cute."

"I know. But listen, why don't you come with us? It would be so much fun. Please?"

"I don't know . . . ," Haley said.

Tori squeezed her arm. "Please come. I—I'm kind of nervous about going out with him alone. I mean, he is older and all. And he's pretty sophisticated."

"I'd like to," Haley said, "but it would be kind of weird. I mean, would he really want me hanging around like a chaperon or something?"

"But Alex will come, too, if you do. So it would be like a double date. I already talked to him about it. Please? You've got to come!"

Alex! A date with Alex. A chance to find out how he felt about her. "Sounds cool," Haley said, trying not to show how excited she really was. Had Tori guessed how she felt about Alex? Was it obvious? she wondered.

Tori gave Haley a quick hug. "I knew I could count on you."

Nikki was out to dinner with her parents and her baby brother that night. All the skaters had put in solid hours of practice that day to be ready for their long programs the next day. But at six o'clock Haley heard Tori knock on their door.

"All set?" Tori asked when Haley let her in. Tori was dressed to party.

"Almost. Does this look okay?" Haley had tried on several different outfits. She had finally decided on leggings and a huge striped shirt.

"That looks great," Tori said, but Haley could tell she wasn't really paying attention. She seemed too nervous about her own date.

"Come on," Tori urged. "We're supposed to meet Pierce at six. And Alex is meeting us downstairs, too. Let's go."

Alex was already waiting by the elevator in the lobby. When he saw them, he smiled. Haley's heart did a little flip inside her chest. Was he feeling what she felt? she wondered.

"So, what movie are we going to see?" she asked.

"Who knows?" Tori answered. "We'll walk to the mall and see what's playing. Alex, have you seen Pierce?"

"Not yet."

Tori gazed around nervously.

"Calm down. He'll be here," Haley said. "This was his idea, wasn't it?"

"There he is." Tori sighed in relief as Pierce hurried toward them.

He was great-looking, Haley had to admit. He was wearing blue jeans, a black T-shirt, and a black suede jacket that went well with his dark hair and eyes.

"Hi, Tori. Ready to go?" Pierce asked.

"Hi, Pierce. This is Haley and Alex. They're from Silver Blades, too. You don't mind if we all go together, do you?"

Haley wasn't sure, but she thought she saw a flicker of annoyance cross his face.

"Fine with me," Pierce said. "Everyone I've met from Silver Blades has been cool. So let's cruise."

They chose a movie that started at seven o'clock. "That gives us time to get something to eat. There's a pizza place across the way. That okay with everyone?" Pierce asked.

"Sounds good to me," Tori said eagerly.

Haley had the feeling that if Pierce had suggested eating bugs and worms, it would have been okay with Tori.

Haley glanced at Alex. "Okay with you?"

"Sure," he replied.

They chose a booth and the waitress took their order. While they waited for a large pizza and drinks, Pierce said, "So, Alex, do you skate singles?"

"No. Pairs. My partner is Nikki Simon."

"I don't know how you guys do it," Pierce said. "That's hard work. Doesn't it get to you?"

"Sometimes. But we really enjoy skating together, so it's worth it," Alex told him.

"You get used to working hard," Haley added. "Do you do any sports?"

"I was on the varsity soccer team last year. I was the only freshman on the team. But I got tired of it," Pierce said. "I didn't go out for it again this year, even though the coach begged me to."

"You made varsity as a freshman?" Tori gaped. "You must be good."

Pierce shrugged. "I guess the coach thought so."

Their food came and Alex helped himself to a slice of pizza. "So what other sports do you like?"

"Tennis and golf," Pierce answered. "I used to play golf with my dad. Then I beat him, and now he won't play anymore."

"Are you on the tennis team at your school?" Haley asked.

Pierce laughed. "The tennis at St. Joseph's is a joke. I wouldn't want to ruin my game by playing in that league. I play at the country club in the summer. At least, I did last year. This summer, who knows? I don't plan to hang around much once I get my driver's license."

"Is that soon?" Tori asked.

"The day I turn sixteen. May twenty-fourth," Pierce replied.

"That's cool. I can't wait till I can drive. But it won't be for years," Haley said.

"Yeah. But I have to talk my mom into buying me a car. I've got my eye on a red Porsche. Then I'll be all set," Pierce boasted.

"Wow. Will she?" Tori asked.

Pierce smiled. "I told her it would be a good incentive for me to get my grades up. She said she'd consider it if I make the honor roll."

"Do you think you will?" asked Haley.

"I made C's without ever opening a book. So it shouldn't be too hard." Pierce smiled at Tori. "You'd look great in a Porsche."

"I would, wouldn't I?" Tori said dreamily.

Haley glanced at Alex. She wondered if he was thinking the same thing she was: This guy was a bit too much.

"So, Haley, you're just here to watch, right? No skating?" Pierce asked.

"Right," Haley said.

"You're, like, a Silver Blades groupie or something?" Pierce joked.

Haley's mouth dropped open.

"Hey, she's one of the best skaters in the club," Alex told Pierce.

"So why aren't you competing?" Pierce asked her.

"I skate pairs. But my partner and I blew it in the Sectionals. We didn't qualify," Haley explained.

"Next year, right, Haley?" Alex raised his hand toward Haley. They slapped a high five.

Pierce glanced at his watch. "It's almost movie time, folks. Are we done?"

As they walked to the theater Pierce told them stories about his boarding school. He was pretty funny, but he sure liked to be the center of attention, Haley thought.

She held Alex back for a second. "What do you think of Pierce?" she whispered.

"Not half as much as he thinks of himself," Alex replied. "Know what I mean?"

Haley nodded. "He does seem kind of high on himself."

"Definitely. And Tori's buying the whole act. She can't take her eyes off him."

As they left the theater after the movie, Pierce said, "Well, it's only nine o'clock. The night is young. What should we do now?"

Haley glanced at Tori. Tori was skating her long program the next day. Haley knew she would want to be rested and ready. Besides, Mrs. Carsen would have a fit if Tori stayed out late.

"We'd better get back," Haley said. "Alex and Tori are both skating their long programs tomorrow. Nikki's already mad at me. She'll kill me if I keep Alex out late."

"Blame it on me. What do I care?" said Pierce. "I say we make a quick stop at Harvey's Hole. It's supposed to be a cool place, and it's right on the way home."

"I don't know," Tori said. "I want to, but I really should get home."

Pierce squeezed her hand. "Look, we *are* going home. We'll just make a quick stop on the way." He checked his watch. "It's only nine o'clock. You'll be in bed at nine-thirty."

Tori bit her lower lip, and Haley could tell she was trying to make up her mind.

"I guess it's fine with me. I don't have to skate tomorrow," Haley said. She had to admit that she wanted to be with Alex as long as possible.

"Well, Mom and Roger won't be back until ten. So as long as we're home before them, I guess it's okay," Tori reasoned. "And maybe it will do us good to relax."

"Right. Sitting around your hotel room worrying won't help any," Pierce told her. "You might as well have some fun." He clapped Alex on the shoulder. "What do you say, Alex? You're not going to wimp out on us, are you?"

Alex shrugged. "I guess a quick stop can't hurt anything. We just won't tell Nikki."

"And we'll pray she doesn't find out!" Haley added.

13

The night air was warm and a light breeze blew as they walked back toward the hotel. "What a beautiful night," Haley said.

"Look at that." Alex pointed at a bright moon that shone through the trees. He took Haley's hand.

"Are you glad you came?" he asked.

"Very," she answered.

"Me too," Alex said.

They strolled along hand in hand. Haley could feel her heart pounding in her chest. He must like me, she told herself. He wouldn't hold my hand if he didn't like me.

"Here's the place I was telling you about," Pierce said. "Harvey's Hole. We'll stop for only a minute."

"As long as it's just a few minutes," Tori agreed.

They went inside and found a booth. When they were settled, Pierce asked, "Anyone want a beer?"

"A beer? I thought this was a coffeehouse," Haley said.

"It is, but they also have beer and wine. Don't you guys ever drink?"

"Our coaches tend to frown on it," Alex joked. "Not to mention our parents."

"They won't serve you if you're under twenty-one, anyway," Tori told him.

Pierce pulled a card out of his wallet and showed it to her. "According to this, I'm twenty-two. Works every time. Sure you don't want me to order you something?"

Tori shook her head. "Just a Coke."

Haley stared at Tori. Did she really like Pierce, even though he was flashing around a fake ID?

"Do you drink a lot?" Haley asked.

Pierce shrugged. "Every chance I get. I'll let you in on a little secret. I'm not really home on semester break. The truth is, I was suspended for drinking on campus."

He sounds as if he's proud of it, Haley thought. Her friends seemed as shocked as she was.

"Everyone does it. But I got caught," he said. "Of course, I'd already gotten away with so much that I was getting kind of careless. From now on I'll have to be more careful."

"From now on? You mean you'll keep on drinking?

Won't they expel you if they catch you again?" Haley asked.

"Yeah, but I won't get caught again," Pierce assured her.

Haley kicked Tori under the table. "Ladies' room," she mouthed.

Tori nodded.

"We'll be right back," Haley told the boys.

As soon as they were out of earshot, Haley whispered, "I can't believe he's going to order a beer. We'd better get out of here. We could get into big trouble."

"Why? We're not drinking. If Pierce wants to have a beer, it's his business." Tori sighed. "Isn't he just the best-looking thing you've ever seen? And he's so . . . I don't know . . . sophisticated."

"Tori, he's bad news. Didn't you hear what he said about being suspended? And it sounds as if it's only a matter of time until he gets expelled."

"Oh, Haley, you're overreacting," Tori declared. "He's almost sixteen. Lots of guys his age drink."

"None that I want to hang out with," Haley said.

"Well, you can stick with those guys if you want. But I'll take Pierce any day."

When they came back from the ladies' room, their drinks had come. Pierce had a beer, and the rest of them had Cokes.

Haley felt very uncomfortable, and she could tell that Alex did, too. She and Alex had been having such a great time. She was mad at Pierce for spoiling it.

She drank her Coke quickly. "Well, I'm sorry for rushing everyone, but I really think we should go. You two do have to skate tomorrow, remember." She glanced at Alex and Tori.

Alex nodded. "We really should get back."

Pierce chugged down his beer, and the others finished their Cokes. They hurried back to the hotel.

It was a few minutes past ten when they entered the lobby.

"Gosh, it's pretty late," Tori said as they headed for the elevators. "I hope my mother's not back yet. She'll be furious if she finds out I just got in."

Pierce put his arm around her. "Wait a minute. Aren't you going to say good night?"

Haley could see that Tori was torn between wanting to stay with Pierce and knowing she had to hurry.

"Come on, Tori. We've really got to run. It's past curfew," Haley reminded her.

"Yeah. We'd better get up to our rooms. Will I see you tomorrow?" Tori asked Pierce.

"Of course you will! I'll be at the rink watching your every move."

The elevator came, and Haley practically had to drag Tori away from Pierce. She shoved her inside before the doors closed.

"Did you hear what he said?" Tori asked. "He'll be watching my every move." She sighed happily.

Alex and Haley exchanged a glance. "Tori, if I were you, I wouldn't get too hung up on him," Alex told her.

"Oh, Alex. You and Haley are acting like babies. Pierce is older and more sophisticated than we are. That's no crime," Tori declared.

"Here's my floor. I'll see you guys tomorrow," Haley said.

"I'll walk you to your room." Alex followed Haley off the elevator.

" 'Night, Tori. Sleep well," Haley called as the doors slid shut.

Alex took Haley's hand as they went down the hall to her room. Haley was nervous. She wondered if he would try to kiss her. She wanted him to, but she was scared.

When they came to her door, Haley fumbled in her bag for her room key while Alex waited. He seemed to want to say something. Haley could tell that he was nervous, too.

"I had a really good time tonight. It's too bad we had to be with that jerk, though," he finally said.

"Yeah. And Tori really likes him. We've got to straighten her out," Haley agreed.

She found her key and unlocked the door. "Well, I guess I'll see you tomorrow, Alex."

"Okay. 'Night, Haley."

" 'Night, Alex." Haley slipped into her room and closed the door behind her. She was a little disappointed that he hadn't kissed her. But at least he had walked her to the room and held her hand. That meant something, didn't it?

The lights in the room were out. Haley whispered, "Nikki? Are you asleep already?"

"I have to skate tomorrow, you know," Nikki grumbled, her voice muffled by the blanket.

"I know. I'm sorry. Did I wake you?" Haley plopped down on the bed.

"I couldn't sleep," Nikki told her. "Was Alex with you all this time?"

"Yes. We had the best time together. He's so much fun."

Haley wanted to tell her all about the evening, but Nikki groaned and rolled over. She pulled the covers up, clearly not interested in what Haley had to say.

"What's wrong? Didn't you have fun with your family?" Haley asked.

"Yes. But I've got the biggest skating event of my life tomorrow. So does Alex. I just want to get some sleep, okay?"

You'd think it was two in the morning, the way she's going on, Haley thought. Oh, well, she told herself. No reason to let Nikki ruin my vacation.

Haley changed into her favorite pajamas. They were old, worn-out shorty pajamas with faded pictures of Mickey Mouse and Goofy on them. She'd had them for years, but she still loved them. Her friends teased her about them, but she planned to keep them until they fell apart.

Since she wasn't ready for bed, she decided it would be a good time to put on her facial mask. The tube said she was supposed to do it once a week, and she hadn't done it for at least two. She had bought the mask at Arnold's department store during her last shopping spree with Tori.

She went into the bathroom, piled her hair on top of her head, and rubbed the green cream onto her face. She glanced at her watch. She was supposed to leave the cream on for twenty minutes. She caught a glimpse of herself in the mirror and laughed. Luckily, no one but Nikki could see her!

While she waited for the cream to work, she sat on the bathroom floor to write a note to Alex wishing him good luck. She was halfway through when the phone rang. She quickly picked it up.

"Haley?"

It was Alex.

"Hi," she said, playing with the phone cord.

"Hi. I had a really good time tonight," Alex said.

"Me too," Haley whispered. As she talked she drew a heart on her foot and wrote "Alex + Haley" inside. He had called her just to tell her he'd had fun that night! Definitely a good sign, Haley thought.

"I'll see you tomorrow, okay?" Alex said.

"Okay."

"Um, Haley, is Nikki there?"

"Nikki?" Why was he asking for Nikki? Hadn't he called to talk to her?

"Yeah. Nikki. You know, your roommate? My skating partner?" he joked.

"Um, Nikki's asleep already, Alex," Haley told him. "Is it important? Should I wake her?"

"No, I just wanted to tell her to get a good night's sleep. I guess it doesn't make much sense to wake her up to tell her that, does it?"

"I guess not," Haley said with a laugh. She was kind of disappointed that he had been calling Nikki and not her.

"Well, I've got to go. I'll see you tomorrow, Haley," Alex said.

"Yeah. 'Night, Alex."

Haley stood up and replaced the receiver. She folded the note she was writing and went into the bedroom. She slid open the drawer of the table that was between the two beds and tucked the note inside.

Nikki groaned and rolled over. "Who was on the phone?" she asked sleepily.

"Oh. You're still awake?" Haley said. "Alex called to tell you to get a good night's sleep."

"I'm trying," Nikki mumbled. "It'd be easier if you weren't making so much noise."

"Well, excuse me. I can't help it if your partner calls you," Haley retorted. She slammed the drawer shut. A pile of magazines slid onto the floor.

"Quit slamming drawers, would you?" Nikki cried.

"Look, this is my room, too. I have the right to open and shut drawers if I want." Haley yanked open the drawer again.

Nikki sat up. "I am sick of you and your rights. I'm

here to skate in the biggest event of my life, and all you've done since you've been here is mess everything up. First you lie to me, and then you distract Alex so he can't concentrate on skating. He's missed tons of jumps lately. Not to mention that you're such a slob it's disgusting!"

Haley couldn't believe what she was hearing. At first she just stared, not saying anything. Then she lost it.

"Well, excuse me for breathing! This is my room, too, you know. If I want my part to be messy, it'll be messy." Haley knocked some clothes off her bed and kicked them. "And as for Alex," Haley went on, "you're the one who's messing up his concentration. You're so uptight about everything. You're here to skate—but it's okay to have a little fun as well. I mean, there's no law against it—not that I know of."

Haley stomped across the room and grabbed the remote control. Then she flopped down on the bed and clicked on the TV. "You know what I think? I think you're jealous. Because Alex likes me instead of you."

Nikki stood up. "I can't believe you said that! That's the dumbest thing I've ever heard. I'm not jealous—I just want to get some sleep. And I'd like to have my partner thinking about our program instead of romance."

Nikki glanced at the note that lay in the open drawer. She saw that it was addressed to Alex. "You can't leave him alone for a minute, can you? You'd think he could have at least tomorrow to think about skating. But no! You have to send him a letter first thing in the morning on the day of our biggest event." She crumpled the letter into a ball. "This is one letter he's never going to get." Nikki flung the door open and threw the letter out into the hall.

"You can't do that!" Haley screamed. "That's my letter and it's personal. Alex is only your skating partner. You don't own him!"

Haley ran into the hall to get the letter. She picked up the crumpled paper and began to smooth it out. She was shaking with anger. Who did Nikki think she was?

The door slammed behind her. Suddenly Haley realized that she was standing out in the hall in her Mickey Mouse shorty pajamas. Her hair was in a messy topknot, and there was sticky green cream all over her face. She whirled around and began pounding on the door.

"Nikki, let me in. Come on, open the door! Nikki, you can't do this!"

She's got to let me in, Haley thought. I can't stand here all night. What if someone walks by?

She began pounding again and yelling. If anyone sees me out here, I'll die, she thought.

Across the hall the elevator door slid open. Out stepped Dr. Lawrence and Pierce.

14

Dear Tori,
Good luck tomorrow! I know we're both going to beat Carla. We're a great team!

Love,
Amber

Amber waited until she was sure her mother was asleep. Then she climbed out of bed, pulled on a pair of jeans, and found her key. She crept out of the room clutching the note. She had wanted to call Tori to say good night, but her mother wouldn't let her. So she had written her a note instead. She was going to slip downstairs to deliver it.

As she closed the door behind her, she heard yelling coming from around the corner. What's going on? she wondered. She hurried down the hall to check it out. She rounded the corner and saw Haley pounding on the door of her room. Haley was dressed in pajamas, her feet were bare, and her hair was pulled up in a really funny way.

"Haley?" Amber called.

When Haley turned toward her, Amber took one look and burst out laughing.

"It's not funny," Haley cried. "Nikki locked me out. I've been out here for ten minutes! And Pierce Lawrence and his father walked by. I could have died. I've never been so embarrassed in my whole life." Haley started pounding on the door again. "I'm going to kill her!"

The elevator doors slid open, and Tori appeared in the hall. She was clutching a huge bag of fat-free popcorn that Haley guessed she wanted to share with her friends. "What's going on, Haley? You're in your pajamas."

"No kidding," Haley said. She spun around. "I've been locked out by my roommate. And I'm going to kill her when she finally opens this door." She pounded on the door between sentences.

Kathy appeared in the hallway. Amber gulped.

"All right, girls. What's going on out here? You're disturbing everyone. What is this all about?" Kathy seemed really upset.

"Nikki locked me out," Haley explained.

Kathy knocked sharply on the door. "Nikki, this is

Kathy. Open the door *immediately*." Amber had never seen her this angry.

The door opened, and Nikki stepped back to let them all in.

"I can't believe you did that to me!" Haley screamed. "I've never been so embarrassed in my whole life." She stomped into the room and caught sight of herself in the mirror. "Look at me. Pierce Lawrence saw me like this!" Amber saw Tori and Nikki glance at each other and snicker. Haley did look funny. Amber started to laugh, too. But Haley didn't think it was a bit funny. She stormed into the bathroom and slammed the door behind her.

"Listen," Kathy said, "it's time we went to bed. Tomorrow's a big day. But before I leave, I want to talk to you all about something. Haley, would you come out here, please?"

"Just a minute," Haley called. A few moments later she hurried out of the bathroom. She had washed the cream off her face and taken her hair down.

Kathy sat down on Nikki's bed. The four girls sat across from her on Haley's. "I just got a call from Dr. Lawrence. Apparently he received some sort of bribe in the hotel mail. He's very upset. It was sent by someone who's also staying in the hotel, and Dr. Lawrence is accusing Silver Blades. Does anyone know anything about this?"

"A bribe? What kind of bribe?" Tori asked.

"Well, the note was pretty vague," Kathy told them.

"It said something like, 'Let me be number one and I'll make it worth your while.' "

Amber gave a little cry and clapped her hand over her mouth. That note! She had read that note in Tori's room. It was the valentine that Mrs. Carsen had written to Roger. But how had it gotten to Dr. Lawrence?

Amber bit her lip. She couldn't tell anyone she recognized the note. Then Tori would know she'd been snooping. And she didn't want Tori to find that out, ever. Tori would never be her friend if she thought Amber was a snoop.

"What's wrong, Amber? You look like you've seen a ghost," Kathy said.

"N-N-Nothing," Amber stammered. "But why does Dr. Lawrence think someone from Silver Blades sent the note?" she asked.

"The desk clerk who delivered the note said so. He remembers that the person who left it at the desk was wearing a Silver Blades jacket," Kathy explained.

"But none of us would bribe a judge," Nikki cried.

"That's what I told him. But I needed to check to make sure that none of you knows anything about it. I'm sure it's all a misunderstanding. I know no one from Silver Blades would do something like that."

Kathy stood up. "We'll straighten this out tomorrow. In the meantime, let's all get some sleep. I'll see you in the morning."

Kathy left, and Tori rose to go. "She's right. We should get to bed. But the strangest things have been happening lately with notes. Like the other night. I sent a valentine to Pierce asking him to meet me. But I don't think he ever got it. Roger showed up instead, saying that Mom had sent him the note I had sent to Pierce. Isn't that weird?" Tori seemed confused.

"And now Dr. Lawrence gets a bribe. This *is* very weird. Maybe someone's trying to frame us," Haley suggested.

"Like who?" Alex asked.

Haley shrugged. "Carla Benson?"

"Even Carla wouldn't sink that low," Nikki declared.

"I guess you're right. But what other explanation is there?" Haley asked.

Nikki shrugged. "All I know is, I've got to get some sleep."

"Me too," Tori agreed. "Good night, everyone."

Amber left with Tori. She had to get out of there. It had suddenly hit her: She was the only one who knew. And it was all her fault. Roger Arnold had gotten the note meant for Pierce. Dr. Lawrence had gotten the note meant for Roger. Amber had accidentally switched them.

It must have happened when she had snooped and read them. She had been scared of being caught, and in her haste she must have stuck the notes into the wrong envelopes. Now Dr. Lawrence thought one of the Silver Blades skaters was trying to bribe him.

As Amber walked back to her room, she felt like crying. If only she weren't so nosy. She had to do something, but what? She couldn't confess. Then Tori would know she had snooped, and she couldn't face that. Not when Tori was just beginning to be her friend. If Tori learned about this, she would never speak to her again.

She couldn't tell her, she just couldn't. She had to think of something else.

Amber paused. She was so upset. She really needed to talk to someone. But she had sneaked out of her room. Could she sneak back in and admit what she'd done?

No way! Amber couldn't face her mom. She'd think Amber couldn't be trusted at all. Dad, Amber decided. I'll call Dad from the pay phone in the lobby.

Amber took the elevator downstairs and went to the row of pay phones. They were all in use. She sat down in the lounge to wait, curling up in one of the big over-stuffed chairs. It was warm in the lounge. In minutes she was sound asleep.

15

Dear Dani,
   Major bulletin! I think Alex really likes me—fi-nally! We had such a great time last night. I am kind of worried, though—his skating has been ter-rible lately. What if he blows it today? Nikki will be furious.
   Keep your fingers crossed—for them and for me.
                                                    Love,
                                                    Haley

Early the next morning, Nikki was grabbing a quick shower. Haley was alone in the bedroom. She folded the note she had just written to Danielle. She was slipping the note into an envelope when someone knocked on the door.

"Just a minute," Haley called.

She went to the door and found Kathy and Mrs. Armstrong waiting outside.

"I need to talk to you for a minute, Haley," her coach said.

"Sure. What's up?" she asked. They both looked worried. "Is anything wrong?"

"We can't find Amber," Mrs. Armstrong cried.

"She didn't sleep in her bed last night. No one seems to know where she is. Do you have any idea?" Kathy asked.

"No. I saw her here last night. She left just after you did, Kathy," Haley answered.

"What about Nikki? Do you think she might know anything?" Mrs. Armstrong asked.

Haley shook her head. "She hasn't been out of the room, either. She's in the shower now. I can ask her if you want, but I don't think she could've seen Amber."

"Well, Nikki has to be at the rink soon. Let's not alarm her before she skates her long program," Kathy advised.

"Have you asked Tori?" Haley asked.

"We're just about to," Kathy told her.

"I'll come with you," Haley decided. "Just a minute."

She hurried back into the room and scribbled a note to Nikki. It said that she and Kathy would meet her at the rink later.

Kathy, Haley, and Mrs. Armstrong hurried down to

Tori's room. Mrs. Carsen was already downstairs eating breakfast with Roger. They explained to Tori what had happened, but she hadn't seen Amber since the night before, either.

"We'd better alert the front desk," Kathy said. "Tori and Haley, why don't you girls go search the rink? Maybe Amber went over there for an early-morning skate."

Kathy turned to Mrs. Armstrong, who looked close to tears. "Don't worry. She'll turn up."

Haley and Tori raced through the lobby and across the road to the arena. They searched the whole place, asking everyone they saw, but no one had seen Amber.

"She's not here. We've been everywhere, and no one's seen her," Haley finally said to Tori.

"Let's head back," Tori suggested. "Maybe they found her in the hotel."

But when they arrived back at the hotel, Kathy was in the lobby talking to a security guard.

"Okay," he was saying, "four feet eight inches tall, brown hair, brown eyes, dressed in jeans and a green sweatshirt. Last seen at about ten-forty-five last evening. Can you think of anything else to add?"

Kathy turned to Haley and Tori. "Did she seem upset to you last night?" she asked.

"Well, she did seem sort of quiet," Haley remembered. "She hardly even said good night."

Haley was beginning to get scared. Where was Amber? It wasn't like her to just disappear. She was usually following them around, always wanting to be with them.

"This is really strange," Haley blurted out.

"Where's Mrs. Armstrong?" Tori asked.

"She was talking to the people in the restaurant to see if any of them had seen Amber last night. Oh, here she comes now," Kathy said.

Mrs. Armstrong's eyes were red from crying. Her voice was faint. "I'm going up to the room and call Amber's father. Maybe he's heard from her," she told them.

"We'll come with you," said Kathy. "And we'll talk about what else we can do."

As they rode the elevator Haley tried to imagine where Amber might have gone. Haley couldn't think of anything. Amber wouldn't leave the hotel alone, would she?

"Have you checked with Dan?" Haley asked. "Maybe she's with him."

"We checked," Kathy said. They hurried down the hall to Mrs. Armstrong's room. "He and Alex were having breakfast in the coffee shop. Neither of them have seen her."

Mrs. Armstrong was about to put her key into the lock when the door suddenly opened. There stood Amber, staring at them curiously. "What are you all doing here?" she asked. "Aren't we supposed to be over at the rink? Nikki's going to be skating soon."

"Amber! Oh, thank heavens! Where on earth have

you been?" Amber's mom threw her arms around her daughter. "We've been looking everywhere for you," she cried.

"You have?"

"Of course! The entire hotel security force is searching for you," Mrs. Armstrong told her. "When I woke up this morning and saw that your bed hadn't been slept in, I didn't know what to think."

Amber gazed at the circle of concerned faces. "You've *all* been looking for *me*?"

"Tori and I searched the skating rink," Haley said. "We thought maybe you'd gone over there without telling anyone."

"We've all been frantic," Kathy added.

"I'm sorry," Amber said. "I went to call Dad last night and I fell asleep in the lounge. I didn't mean to cause so much trouble. I didn't think anyone but Mom would care where I was."

"What do you mean, Amber? Of course we care," Kathy said. "All of us."

Amber shrugged.

"You think we don't care about you?" Haley asked.

Suddenly Amber started to cry. "I know you guys don't really like me. You just let me hang out with you because Kathy makes you. And because I get all the interviews," she said, looking right at Tori.

Haley and Tori exchanged glances. Haley wondered if Tori felt as awful as she did. If what Amber said was true, they had been pretty mean to her.

"But we do like you, Amber. It's just that . . . well, you *are* kind of pushy sometimes," Tori tried to explain.

"But we still like you a lot," Haley reassured her.

Amber cried even harder.

"Honey, what is it? What's wrong?" Mrs. Armstrong asked. She threw an arm around her daughter.

"I've done something bad," Amber admitted.

"What do you mean?" Kathy asked.

"You know how Dr. Lawrence thought someone was bribing him?" Amber asked.

"Surely you didn't have anything to do with that," Kathy said.

"I didn't mean to. But it's all my fault," Amber confessed.

"How? Did you send him the note?" Tori asked.

"No," Amber said. "I got the valentines mixed up."

"Amber, you're not making any sense. How do valentines have anything to do with a bribe?" her mother asked.

Amber explained how the valentines had gotten mixed up in their envelopes.

"Of course!" Kathy exclaimed. "Dr. Lawrence and Pierce have the same first name. So the judge assumed that Tori's note addressed to Pierce was for him."

Amber reminded them of what Mrs. Carsen's note

said: "Let me be your number one and you won't re-gret it." Finally they all understood what had hap-pened.

"I didn't mean to snoop. I know it was wrong, but I couldn't help myself. I'm really sorry," Amber apol-ogized.

"It's okay. I've done stuff like that before," Tori said.

"You forgive me?"

"Sure." Tori gave Amber a hug.

"But what is Dr. Lawrence going to do?" Amber asked, sniffling.

"Well, I'll call him and explain what happened." Ka-thy put an arm around Amber. "When he hears it was all a mistake, I'm sure he'll understand."

Amber was still crying. "I just feel so bad. I should have explained last night, when I realized what had happened. But I was afraid you'd kick me out of Silver Blades if I told."

"Kick you out of Silver Blades?" Kathy knelt down, placing one hand on each of Amber's shoulders. "Am-ber, we're a team. You're an important member of our team. And that's the way it's going to stay. Under-stand?"

Amber nodded. Haley handed her some tissues, and she blew her nose.

"Now the mystery of the bribe is solved. So all you guys have to do is skate your very best," Kathy said. She stood up and clapped her hands for attention, becoming the firm coach they knew so well. "It's time we got to the rink. Let's get moving, everyone."

"Well, I guess everything's back to normal," Haley joked. "Kathy's yelling at us—just like she always does."

16

"This is it!" Haley grabbed Tori's hands and then Amber's. The three of them sat together in the stands. Tori felt as nervous as if she were about to skate herself.

Then Alex's and Nikki's names were announced.

They skated smoothly into the center of the rink. Their music began.

They were both smiling, but only Alex's smile seemed genuine. Something about Nikki's expression told Haley that she was very nervous. She'll relax as they get going, Haley told herself.

They were skating well, executing some difficult jumps and spins and going through the footwork segments with precise, well-timed moves. But still Nikki's performance seemed stiff. Maybe no one else will notice, Haley thought. And technically they're doing great.

Halfway through their program they had a lasso lift. Nikki swung her leg around too wildly and wobbled badly.

Haley's fingers tightened. She, Amber, and Tori drew in simultaneous breaths. They exhaled with relief when Nikki recovered and skated into her next move.

"Whew. That was close," Tori whispered. "It's lucky Alex caught her, but she'll still lose two tenths of a point."

After that it seemed as though Nikki was having trouble regaining her composure. They were skating back crossovers. Haley knew that they were supposed to go into a split double twist, but they must have decided not to try it. Instead they substituted another footwork segment. Then they glided into the finale, which included a death spiral and a side-by-side flying camel. They completed both moves successfully. But their performance lacked the smooth fluidity that they usually showed.

Nikki seemed crushed as she and Alex skated off the ice. Haley, Tori, and Amber hugged them and told them they had done well. But it was obvious that Nikki knew the truth.

"I blew it," Nikki admitted. "I was too nervous. I kept thinking I'd relax once we got going, but I never did. And then when I almost fell, I couldn't get my focus back." She turned to her partner. "I'm really sorry, Alex."

"Hey, it was my fault as much as yours. My timing was off on that lasso," he said.

"No, I'm the one who blew it. And all week I've been blaming you and Haley. I guess I was afraid to admit I felt shaky. I'm sorry, you guys." She looked directly at Haley, and Haley hugged her again. She was just so glad that Nikki wasn't mad anymore.

The numbers came up. They were disappointing, placing Alex and Nikki in the lowest third of the pairs skaters.

Dan was careful to be reassuring. "That's okay," he said. "Very respectable for your first time in the Nationals. You'll have plenty of chances to try again. Look at it this way—how many kids make it to Nationals to begin with? You should be very proud of yourselves."

"I'm just glad it's over," Nikki declared. "I've never been so worried about anything in my whole life."

"I'm kind of glad, too. Now we've got the real Nikki back. I was beginning to think I was living with the roommate from outer space," Haley teased.

"Well, you're no prize yourself, considering I can't see the floor on your half of the room because it's covered with your clothes." Nikki grinned. "Seriously, I'm sorry, Haley. Especially for locking you out and all."

Tori started to laugh. "You did look pretty funny banging away on that door in your pajamas."

"Especially with that cream all over your face," added Amber.

"When you think about it, it really was pretty funny," Nikki said.

Even Haley started laughing. "I thought I was going to die when Pierce and his father walked by. Do you think they recognized me?"

"Your own mother wouldn't recognize you like that!" Tori laughed.

Kathy came over to tell Tori and Amber that it was time to get ready for their event. But they were all laughing so hard, they were crying.

"What's going on?" Kathy asked.

"We were just wondering what Pierce and his father thought when they saw Haley in the hall in her pajamas last night," Tori explained.

Kathy grinned. "You were quite a sight," she agreed.

"Hey," Nikki cried. "Speaking of Pierce, isn't that him up there in the stands?"

"Where?" Tori turned to gaze in the direction that Nikki was pointing.

"Right up there, beside that—Oops," Nikki blurted out, glancing at Tori.

Pierce was there all right. Next to him was the girl they had seen him with in the coffee shop. Pierce had his arm around her, and he was laughing at something she said.

"That's the girl he was with the other night," Haley said. "Didn't he tell us she was a friend of the family?"

"That's what he said, but . . ." As Tori stared, Pierce drew the girl closer and kissed her lightly.

Haley squeezed Tori's hand. "I told you. That guy is bad news."

Tori forced a smile. "Well, it's no trouble for me to forget him. He wasn't so great anyway."

"Not half as great as you are," Amber told Tori.

"She's right," Haley said. "And when you and Amber beat Carla Benson this afternoon, you'll be the best!"

17

Dear Amber,
*   Good luck! Let's show Carla Benson what we*
can do! From your teammate and friend,

Tori

This was it—the moment Tori had been waiting for all week. Well, for years, actually. Soon she would be skating her long program at the Nationals. Soon she would beat Carla Benson.

Tori was still fuming that Carla was in fifth place going into the event while Tori had placed sixth. She wished she hadn't almost touched down landing her triple loop. It was even more embarrassing that Amber had placed fourth, ahead of both Carla and Tori.

But anything can happen in the long program, Tori reminded herself.

"Hurry up, Tori. We need to get over to the rink with plenty of time to spare. I don't want you to feel rushed once you're there," her mother called.

"Just let me finish this note to Amber," Tori said.

"Why are you writing her a note? You'll see her in person in a few minutes."

"I know, but I need to do this," Tori tried to explain. "I'll be skating against Amber today, too. Before I do, I want her to know I'm really her friend."

"Well, that's very nice, but you've got other things to think about. Now, where are the tights that you're going to wear? I know they were here."

"I've got them on, Mom." Tori sighed. Her mother was going to drive her crazy, she was sure of it.

"Oh yes, of course. We'd better do your hair. I'd rather do it now than later."

"But all I have to do is pull it back and fasten the ribbon in place. We can wait till we get to the rink for that."

"Well, have we got your new laces? Are your skates polished?" Mrs. Carsen asked.

"Mom, my skates are all ready. You've checked them three times."

"I just want to make sure everything's in order."

There was a knock on the door, and her mother answered it.

"Hello, ladies. Are we ready?" It was Roger.

"Almost," said Mrs. Carsen. "I haven't spoken to Dan yet about Tori's music. I'm not sure he delivered it to the correct person this morning."

"Mom, please!" Tori interrupted. "We've been over all this stuff a hundred times. You have to calm down. You're making me nervous. How can I relax when you're acting like this?" Tori cast a glance at Roger and rolled her eyes.

Roger put his arm around Mrs. Carsen's waist. "Honey, why don't you and I go on over to the rink? Maybe Tori needs a few minutes to herself," he suggested.

"But we always go together. She might be late if we leave her here," her mother said.

"I think Tori can manage to get there on her own," Roger assured her.

"I can, Mom. Please go on ahead. I'll be right over, I promise."

"Well, if you're sure . . ." Mrs. Carsen paused and gazed at Tori.

"I'm positive," Tori said.

Roger helped Mrs. Carsen gather up her things. "Let's see—key, purse, camera, jacket . . . What else, Roger?"

"I think that's everything," Roger answered.

Tori smiled. It was sort of nice the way her mother relied on him. Her mother had never relied on anyone before. Roger put his arm on Mrs. Carsen's shoulder and ushered her toward the door. Suddenly Tori rushed over and gave her mother a hug and a kiss.

"Good luck, darling," her mother told her. "We'll be rooting for you. I know you'll do beautifully! Be sure to tie the new laces firmly, though."

"Mom!" Tori exclaimed.

"Come on, Corinne. We want to be sure to get good seats." Roger practically shoved Tori's mother out the door.

As soon as they were gone Tori breathed a sigh of relief. I never thought I'd say this, she told herself, but thank heavens for Roger.

Tori glanced at her watch. She still had fifteen minutes before she was supposed to meet Dan at the rink. Dan was always talking about visualizing. He had shown her how to imagine herself skating her best. Maybe she should try it his way.

Tori sat down and closed her eyes. She ran through her whole program in her mind, imagining that she was skating her very best. When she was through, she felt relaxed and confident. She was still nervous, but not nearly as nervous as she had been. Maybe this stuff really does work, she thought.

Amber was one of the first skaters in the afternoon event. Tori had arrived at the rink in plenty of time to watch her program. Tori herself would be skating last. Usually she wouldn't watch a skater perform right before she had to perform herself, but this was a special case. She just had to know how well Amber skated. Tori hurried to a bench behind the rink just as Amber took the ice.

Amber may have been the youngest one there, but her skating was strong and mature. And she was so brave. She had to be scared, but if she was, it didn't show. She was skating beautifully. She captured and held the audience's attention. She executed one perfectly timed move after another. When it was over, the applause was thunderous.

She skated off the ice, and Tori rushed to congratulate her. Amber beamed when Tori gave her a big hug.

"You did great," Tori praised her. "Nice work!"

"Really?" Amber asked. She couldn't hide her pleasure at Tori's attention. Tori thought it was kind of cute. It really means a lot to her that I care about her, Tori realized.

"Really," Tori told her. "The audience was hanging on your every move."

Then the scores came up.

"Yes!" Tori screamed. She squeezed Amber tightly. She was so excited. Amber had done really well. Could she possibly beat Carla?

And will I do as well? Tori wondered. She was glad someone in Silver Blades might beat Carla. If it had to be Amber, that was okay. But it would be much better to beat Carla herself. And Tori wanted to beat Amber, too.

It was Carla's turn next. Tori couldn't bear to watch, but when Carla was finished skating, Amber rushed to tell her what had happened.

At first Carla had performed an almost flawless program. But then she had touched down twice, and she'd doubled her triple flip. It looked as if Amber had beaten her.

Finally it was Tori's turn to skate. She took a deep breath and glanced at Dan.

"I'm a little scared," she whispered.

"Of course you are," he said calmly. "Who wouldn't be? But you know your program. All you have to do is go out there and skate. Just like you did yesterday and the day before that and the day before that. That's all. Nothing else. Just skate. If I'm not mistaken, skating is what you do best, right?"

Tori grinned. He was right. Skating was what she did best.

They announced her name, and her music started. Tori felt a burst of energy. She was good—and she wanted everyone to know it.

Her program flew by. She performed the opening moves, then sailed into the slower middle segment. She performed her double axel flawlessly! As she prepared for the finish she went smoothly from the triple lutz into a flying camel. Then she performed her final move, a sit spin.

She heard the applause begin. Her mother and Roger were standing up and clapping. Nikki and Alex were standing, too. Behind the barrier, Amber, Dan, and Kathy were cheering for her. It was all over. She had done it! She had skated in the Nationals, and she had done her best.

She glided off the ice. She had never felt better in her life. She almost didn't care what her score was. She knew she had skated her very best.

But when her marks came up, they were fantastic. Moments later, the announcer's voice boomed over the loudspeaker.

"Ladies and Gentlemen, we have our medalists," he told the crowd. First, he named the gold- and silver-medal winners. Tori held her breath the whole time.

". . . and taking home the bronze medal is—Tori Carsen!"

Tori gasped. Beside her, Dan cheered and punched the air. "Yes!" he shouted.

She had finished third!

She had beaten Carla Benson and Amber!

Carla had come in seventh. And Amber had placed sixth. She, Tori Carsen, who was skating in the Junior Nationals for the very first time, had placed third! She was going home with the bronze medal!

18

It was their last night in San Jose. Tori could hardly believe it. They had been preparing for this trip for months, and now it was all over. They were leaving on an early plane the next morning. Tori decided to pack that night. She had just begun packing the first bag when the phone rang.

"Are you ready?" It was Amber. "The party starts in five minutes. Can I come over to your room so we can go together?"

Tori raised her eyebrows. Ever since she'd sent that valentine, Amber had followed her everywhere. She wanted to be with Tori whenever she could. Tori understood how important it was to Amber to have a friend. The truth was, she really didn't mind. Tori was sort of flattered by her hero worship.

"Sure," Tori said. "I'm packing up now so that I won't have to worry about it later. Come on up."

A minute later there was a knock on the door.

"It's open," Tori called. Amber appeared in the doorway.

"Are you ready for the party?" Amber asked.

"Almost." Tori checked the mirror. Suddenly she reached out, picked up the bronze medal, and hung it around her neck. She gave her hair a final brushing.

"Oh, let me see." Amber leaned close to Tori and examined the medal.

"Want to try it on?" Tori asked.

Amber's eyes lit up. "Yes!" Tori removed the medal and handed it to Amber. Amber held her breath as she placed the ribbon around her neck. She gazed at herself in the mirror for a long time. Finally she handed it back to Tori.

"Maybe you'll have one of your own someday," Tori told her.

Amber grinned. "I hope!" She glanced around the room. "Where's your mom?"

"She and Roger are going to have dinner and then stop by the party."

The party was down the hall in Kathy's room. Almost everyone else was already there when Amber and Tori arrived.

"Here they are," Nikki cried when she saw them. "We were wondering where you guys were. You've got to sign the valentine." She pointed to a large paper banner hanging across Kathy's door. Hearts were drawn along its border. Across the middle was written, "We left our hearts in San Jose."

"What's that for?" Tori asked.

"Dan wants to take a big group picture of us tomorrow morning. It's for our Silver Blades scrapbook," Nikki explained.

"We're going to hold the banner in the photo," Haley added. She glanced shyly at Alex. "So we'll always remember the Nationals and this Valentine's Day."

"Just another piece of Silver Blades history," Nikki said, quoting one of Dan's favorite sayings.

Tori grinned. She didn't mind the idea of a group photo at all. She could wear her medal.

"I love it," Tori exclaimed. She and Amber signed their names underneath Alex's and Nikki's.

"We're supposed to meet Dan outside the rink first thing in the morning," Nikki said.

"That'll be perfect," Tori declared.

Haley took Tori's arm and drew her aside. "Guess what?" she whispered. "This really is a special Valentine's Day. Alex asked me to go to the movies with him when we get back to Seneca Hills."

"He asked you out?" Tori cried.

Haley nodded, and Tori gave her a huge squeeze.

Alex came over and took Haley's hand. "Come on, Haley. You haven't signed the valentine yet." He led her to the banner and handed her a pen.

The door burst open. Mrs. Carsen appeared with Roger at her side.

"Look, everyone!" Tori's mother raised her hand. A glistening diamond ring caught the light. "We're engaged!" Everyone crowded close.

Amber sighed. "It's so romantic, getting engaged on Valentine's Day."

Tori hugged her mother. "Congratulations, Mom," she said. Roger bent down and Tori gave him a kiss on the cheek. "Congratulations," she repeated. She had to admit, Roger was good for her mother. And they did seem happy together. Even if getting engaged on Valentine's Day was pretty corny.

"Too bad things didn't work out with you and Pierce," Amber told her when Tori stepped aside.

"Well, he was cute. But he was a big jerk," Tori said. "Remember to watch out for that, Amber. And anyway," she said with a smile, "I think I may have another valentine."

"You do? Who?" Amber asked.

"A secret admirer," Tori answered.

"Did he send you a valentine?"

Tori nodded. "Isn't it romantic?" She sighed loudly. "He didn't even sign his name. Too shy, I guess."

"That's weird," Amber said. "I got a valentine from a secret admirer, too. It said, 'Keep your heart set on your goal.'"

"So did mine!" Tori cried.

"I got one of those, too," Nikki added.

"Me too," Alex said.

"We all got the same valentine? From the same secret admirer?" Nikki's mouth dropped open.

"Wait a minute," Tori said. "You mean, everyone got one? It wasn't just me?"

Nikki threw her arm around Tori's shoulder. "Sorry for bursting your bubble."

"But who sent them?" Tori asked.

Nikki shrugged. "I guess it's a big Valentine's Day mystery."

Kathy frowned. "Well, I think I have an idea—"

At that moment Dan burst into the room. "If anyone ever earned a party, it's you guys. What a team!" He put one arm around Tori and the other around Amber. "See what you can accomplish when you keep your heart set on your goal?"

For a moment no one said a word. Then the room exploded with laughter.

"What's the joke? Did I say something funny?" Dan seemed bewildered.

When they finally stopped laughing, Tori said, "No! We were just trying to figure out who sent the valentines."

"Tori thought she had a secret admirer," Alex explained to Dan.

Dan smacked his forehead. "Oops! Sorry for getting your hopes up, Tori," he said. "It was just old Dan, trying to inspire you to skate your best."

"Well, I guess it worked." Tori grinned. "We all did pretty well!"

At six o'clock the next morning, Nikki, Haley, Amber, Alex, and Tori stood outside the ice arena. They were all holding the valentine banner.

"I wonder where Dan is." Tori glanced around the open area. "The van for the airport leaves in fifteen minutes."

"Well, here's the tree," Amber said. "He said to meet him right here."

"Hey—I have an idea! Let's hang the valentine from that big branch." Haley pointed up at the tree. "It can be in the photo and we can all stand under it."

"That sounds great!" Tori exclaimed. "Leave it to you, Haley."

Haley beamed with pride. "Sure. We can even leave it hanging there when we leave. Then everyone will remember Silver Blades was at the Nationals."

"If we hang it high enough, they won't be able to get it down for a few days," Tori added. "Should we vote on it?"

Everyone in the group shouted yes. They trooped over to the tree.

"Alex, give me a leg up. I can climb this easily," Haley said.

Alex boosted her up into the tree. Haley climbed to the thick branch that hung out over the walkway.

"Perfect. Tie it on that branch right there," Tori called.

Haley shimmied out onto the branch and reached down for the valentine. Alex held it up as high as he could, but she was too high up.

"You'll have to bring it up," Haley told him.

"I'll send Amber," Alex said. "Come on, Amber. Up you go."

He boosted her into the tree and then gave her the valentine. Amber climbed up to where Haley was waiting and handed it to her.

"Great. Now all we need is the string. Did you bring it with you?"

Amber shook her head.

"We need string," Haley shouted down to the others.

Tori pulled a long piece of string and some tape out of her pocket. "I have it right here," she said. "Should I try to toss it up?"

"You'll never make it. You'll have to climb up, too."

So Alex gave Tori a boost.

Amber, Haley, and Tori began attaching the string to the valentine. "Put plenty of tape on it. We want it to be here for a while," Alex reminded them.

Suddenly Haley shrieked as the valentine slipped out of her hands and fluttered down to the ground. "I dropped it," she cried.

Nikki raced to grab the valentine before it blew away. She glanced at Alex. "Who's next? You or me?"

"I'll go." Alex grasped the paper banner and began to climb up to the others.

"We need a picture of this! Lucky for us, I brought my camera," Nikki said. She had just pulled the camera out of her pocket when the tape landed at her feet.

"Nikki . . ."

"I know," she said. "I'm coming up." She set her camera down underneath the tree. She grabbed the tape and pulled herself onto the lower branch. Then she climbed up to the others.

They were so busy trying to hang the valentine that no one noticed the security guard until he said, "Haven't I seen you folks somewhere before?" He was standing underneath the tree staring up at them. "You look mighty familiar."

Tori swallowed hard. It was the same security guard who had let them skate their first night in San Jose.

"Would you mind telling me what you're all doing in that tree?" he demanded.

"Uh . . . we were just trying to hang this valentine. It's a token of our appreciation," Alex explained.

"I've got to see this," the guard muttered. He waited while they finished tying the string to the branch. They let go of the valentine banner. It swung out over the walkway where everyone could see it.

"Perfect!" Haley cried.

" 'We left our hearts in San Jose,' " the guard read. " 'Love from Silver Blades.' Ah yes. Now I remember where I've seen you all before." The guard winked. "You all skated pretty well, from what I heard. I guess it can't hurt anything to hang that banner," he added.

"Our coaches will be here soon to take a picture of it," Amber told him.

"As long as we're up here and you're down there, would you do us a favor?" Tori asked.

"Depends," said the guard.

She pointed to the camera. "Would you mind taking a picture now?"

He grinned and picked up the camera. "My pleasure."

"Make sure you get us all in," Haley cried.

"And the banner. Get that in, too," Alex added.

The guard lifted the camera and focused. Tori, Amber, Nikki, Haley, and Alex crowded close together.

"Silver Blades," the guard mumbled as he snapped the picture. "Quite a team, Silver Blades. Quite a team."

**Don't miss any of the previous books in
the Silver Blades series:**

#1: Breaking the Ice

Nikki Simon is thrilled when she makes the Silver Blades skating club. But Nikki quickly realizes that being a member of Silver Blades is going to be tougher than she thought. Both Nikki and another skater, Tori Carsen, have to land the double flip jump. But how far will Tori go to make sure *she* lands it first?

#2: In the Spotlight

Danielle Panati has always worked hard at her skating, and it's definitely starting to pay off. Danielle's just won the lead role in the Silver Blades Fall Ice Spectacular. Rehearsals go well at first; then the other members of Silver Blades start noticing that Danielle is acting strange. Is it the pressure of being in the spotlight—or does Danielle have a secret she doesn't want to share?

#3: The Competition

Tori Carsen loves skating when her mother isn't around, but as soon as her mother appears at the rink, skating becomes a nightmare. Mrs. Carsen argues with Tori's coaches and embarrasses her in front of the rest of the club. When Tori and several other members of Silver Blades go to Lake Placid for a regional competition, her mother becomes even more demanding. Could it have anything to do with a mysterious stranger who keeps showing up at the rink?

#4: Going for the Gold

It's a dream come true! Jill's going to the famous figure-skating center in Colorado. But the training is *much* tougher than Jill ever expected, and Kevin, a really cute skater at the school, has a plan that's sure to get her into *big* trouble. Could this be the end of Jill's skating career?

#5: The Perfect Pair

Nikki Simon and Alex Beekman are the perfect pair on the ice. But off the ice there's a big problem. Suddenly Alex is sending Nikki gifts and asking her out on dates. Nikki wants to be Alex's partner in pairs but not his girlfriend. Will she lose Alex when she tells him? Can Nikki's friends in Silver Blades find a way to save her friendship with Alex *and* her skating career?

#6: Skating Camp

Summer's here and Jill Wong can't wait to join her best friends from Silver Blades at skating camp. It's going to be just like old times. But things have changed since Jill left Silver Blades to train at a famous ice academy. Tori and Danielle are spending all their time with another skater, Haley Arthur, and Nikki has a big secret that she won't share with anyone. Has Jill lost her best friends forever?

#7: The Ice Princess

Tori's favorite skating superstar, Elyse Taylor, is in town, and she's staying with Tori! When Elyse promises to teach Tori her famous spin, Tori's sure they'll become the best of friends. But Elyse isn't the sweet champion everyone thinks she is. And she's going to make problems for Tori!

#8: Rumors at the Rink

Haley can't believe it—Kathy Bart, her favorite coach in the whole world, is quitting Silver Blades! Haley's sure it's all her fault. Why didn't she listen when everyone told her to stop playing practical jokes on Kathy? With Kathy gone, Haley knows she'll never win the next big competition. She has to make Kathy change her mind—no matter what. But will Haley's secret plan work?

#9: Spring Break

Jill is home from the Ice Academy, and everyone is treating her like a star. And she loves it! It's like a dream come true—especially when she meets cute, fifteen-year-old Ryan McKensey. He's so fun and cool—and he happens to be her number-one fan! The only problem is that he doesn't understand what it takes to be a professional athlete. Jill doesn't want to ruin her chances with such a great guy. But will dating Ryan destroy her future as an Olympic skater?

#10: Center Ice

It's gold medal time for Tori—she just knows it! The next big competition is coming up, and Tori has a winning routine. Now all she needs is that fabulous skating dress her mother promised her! But Mrs. Carsen doesn't seem to be interested in Tori's skating anymore—not since she started dating a new man in town. When Mrs. Carsen tells Tori she's not going to the competition, Tori decides enough is enough! She has a plan that will change everything—forever!

#11: A Surprise Twist

Danielle's on top of the world! All her hard work at the rink has paid off. She's good. Very good. And Dani's new English teacher, Ms. Howard, says she has a real flair for writing—she might even be the best writer in her class. Trouble is, there's a big skating competition coming up—*and* a writing contest. Dani's stumped. Her friends and family are counting on her to skate her best. But Ms. Howard is counting on her to write a winning story. How can Dani choose between skating and her new passion?

#12: The Winning Spirit

A group of Special Olympics skaters is on the way to Seneca Hills! The skaters are going to pair up with the Silver Blades members in a minicompetition. Everyone in Silver Blades thinks Nikki Simon is really lucky—her Special Olympics partner is Carrie, a girl with Down syndrome who's one of the best visiting skaters. But Nikki can't seem to warm up to the idea of skating with Carrie. In fact, she seems to be hiding something . . . but what?

#13: The Big Audition

Holiday excitement is in the air! Jill Wong, one of Silver Blades' best skaters, is certain she will win the leading role of Clara in the *Nutcracker on Ice* spectacular—until young skater Amber Armstrong comes along. At first Jill can't believe that Amber is serious competition. But she had better believe it—and fast! Because she's about to find herself completely out of the spotlight.

#14: Nutcracker on Ice

Nothing is going Jill Wong's way. She hates her role in the *Nutcracker on Ice* spectacular. And she's hardly on the ice long enough to be noticed! To top it all off, the Ice Academy coaches seem awfully impressed with Jill's main rival, Amber Armstrong. Jill has worked so hard to return to the Academy, and now she might lose her chance. Does Jill have what it takes to save her lifelong dream?

Do you have a younger brother or sister? Maybe he or she would like to meet Jill Wong's little sister Randi and her friends in the exciting new series SILVER BLADES FIGURE EIGHTS. Look for these titles at your bookstore or library:

ICE DREAMS
STAR FOR A DAY

and coming soon:

THE BEST ICE SHOW EVER!
BOSSY ANNA